HOEYE, Michael

No time like show time

'An endearing m[...] [...]y [and] sharp modern w[...]

'A chic, distinctive, offbeat thriller' – Observer

'I have a new hero. It is Hermux Tantamoq . . . I cannot commend my new hero and his author highly enough' – *Bookseller*

'A slick, unusual and sophisticated tale. Talking animals usually leave me cold but this is different . . . a marvellous, twisting and turning detective story. Time flies with this one . . . A real find' – *Irish Times*

Praise for *The Sands of Time*, the second
Hermux Tantamoq Adventure

'[Hermux Tantamoq] charmed his way into the hearts of readers' – *TES*

'This is a whisker-filled Indiana Jones-style page-turner with hero Hermux proving once again that he's the mouse with nous!' – *Funday Times*

'Although I confess to being utterly beguiled by Hermux's pet ladybird, Terfle, the themes of history, perception, civilization and exploitation punch way above a mouse's weight, and Hoeye's language is a joy throughout' – *Daily Telegraph*

'For those of you who have not yet encountered my hero Hermux Tantamoq, I suggest you admire him in his latest courageous expedition . . . Michael Hoeye's excellent, offbeat, tales of scandal, mystery, mice and adventure. Cats beware . . .' – *Bookseller*

'Lots of neat twists and scary cliffhangers' – *Herald*

No Time Like Show Time

A HERMUX TANTAMOQ ADVENTURE®

MICHAEL HOEYE

PUFFIN

Other Hermux Tantamoq Adventures
by Michael Hoeye

Time Stops for No Mouse
The Sands of Time

To DAVID VOGEL
for your support, your vision,
and your storytelling
and
to LARRY FULTON
for your humor,
your unending patience,
and for giving me the title of this book.

Without both of you,
this book would never have happened.

PUFFIN BOOKS

Published by the Penguin Group
Penguin Books Ltd, 80 Strand, London WC2R 0RL, England
Penguin Group (USA) Inc., 375 Hudson Street, New York, New York 10014, USA
Penguin Group (Canada), 90 Eglinton Avenue East, Suite 700, Toronto, Ontario, Canada M4P 2Y3
(a division of Pearson Penguin Canada Inc.)
Penguin Ireland, 25 St Stephen's Green, Dublin 2, Ireland (a division of Penguin Books Ltd)
Penguin Group (Australia), 250 Camberwell Road, Camberwell, Victoria 3124, Australia
(a division of Pearson Australia Group Pty Ltd)
Penguin Books India Pvt Ltd, 11 Community Centre, Panchsheel Park, New Delhi – 110 017, India
Penguin Group (NZ), cnr Airborne and Rosedale Roads, Albany, Auckland 1310, New Zealand
(a division of Pearson New Zealand Ltd)
Penguin Books (South Africa) (Pty) Ltd, 24 Sturdee Avenue, Rosebank, Johannesburg 2196, South Africa

Penguin Books Ltd, Registered Offices: 80 Strand, London WC2R 0RL, England

www.penguin.com

First published in the USA by G.P. Putnam's Sons,
a division of Penguin Group (USA), Inc. 2004
First published in Great Britain in Puffin Books 2004
Published in this edition 2006

2

Text copyright © Michael Hoeye, 2004
A Hermux Tantamoq Adventure is a Registered trademark, and
Rated: Not Too Scary is a servicemark of Terfle House Limited.

The moral right of the author has been asserted

Set in Cochin
Made and printed in England by Clays Ltd, St Ives plc

British Library Cataloguing in Publication Data
A CIP catalogue record for this book is available from the British Library

ISBN-13: 978-0-141-31514-0
ISBN-10: 0-141-31514-8

Contents

Chapter 1
BELLS ARE RINGING

Hermux Tantamoq closed his eyes and listened. Amidst the general ticking and tocking of his watch shop, he heard a whir followed by two tiny clicks. A mouse with a less precise sense of time and with a less sensitive ear probably wouldn't have heard it. And one with a less detailed understanding of mechanisms wouldn't have known what it was.

But Hermux knew it was his grandfather's great longcase clock preparing to strike the second hour of the afternoon. The deep gong sounded once. Twice. Then, from every table, shelf and corner of the shop, the other clocks joined in. Bells rang. Cymbals banged. Chimes clanged. It was a messy and altogether lovely sound. It made Hermux smile, although he made a mental note to himself. The mantel clock with the little sailboat that rocked back and forth on blue tin waves was three seconds late. He would need to adjust that as soon as he had had his afternoon cup of tea.

But first things first! The day was more than half over, and Hermux had something very important to do that couldn't wait. He walked back to his workshop. There on the wall behind his very neat workbench was pinned a large calendar from the

1

International Cheese Society. The month of May featured a handsome wedge of creamy Camembert.

Hermux used a black crayon to draw an X over the date of the eighteenth. 'The very last day,' he said with satisfaction.

On the calendar the next day was boldly circled in red. But a careful observer might have noticed that the circle tended ever so slightly towards a heart shape. It was the day that Linka Perflinger – adventuress, daredevil, aviatrix and Hermux's special friend – was scheduled to return from her latest trip.

Hermux could hardly wait.

He put on the kettle for tea, put a tea bag in his favourite mug, and chose two cookies from the cookie tin. He checked his pocket watch. It was nine minutes after two o'clock. He listened for the door. At ten minutes after, the door of the shop opened and closed.

'Hermux? Are you here?'

It was the postlady, Lista Blenwipple. As usual she was on time. Hermux and Lista both appreciated punctuality.

'Something special for you!' sang Lista.

'What is it?' asked Hermux from the doorway.

'A postcard. From Linka!'

'Oh,' said Hermux, trying to sound cool and calm.

'But I suppose you'd like to start with the magazines and bills.'

'No,' said Hermux firmly. 'The postcard.'

'It's got a wonderful photograph of a volcano!' Lista told him. She held the card out so Hermux could see it. 'Mount Brimminy. It's twelve thousand feet tall. And it blows up all the time. I hope she didn't have to land too close.'

'May I see the card?' Hermux asked.

Lista surrendered it.

2

'Gosh!' said Hermux. 'Look at that lava.'

'Go ahead and read it, Hermux. Don't mind me.'

'I don't want to hold you up.'

'I've got plenty of time.' Lista was not leaving.

Hermux turned the card over, but before he could begin to read, Lista recited it from memory.

Dear Hermux,

The trip has gone very well so far. We have visited 12 of the Fanooshian Islands. Good flying. Clear weather. Markets full. Mr and Mrs Knilloquick have had great success with their stick collecting. I see now why some people call them pack-rats. The plane is nearly full and we still have 6 more islands to go. Yesterday I found a wonderful stick for you. It's very primitive and painted with black and white zigzags. It would look nice over your mantel. We start home in a week, and we should arrive on schedule.

My best to Terfle. And 2 U.

Linka

P.S. Mt Brimminy is magnificent. Even more beautiful than the picture!

Just then the kettle whistled.

'She writes a charming card,' said Lista. She dumped the rest of Hermux's mail on the counter and started towards the door. She would have to walk fast to get to Lanayda Prink's coffee shop before the 2:20 rush. Lista wanted the centre seat at the counter so she could be heard when she gave her performance of Linka's postcard. It was good that she had got the chance to rehearse. Then there was the business of Cladenda Noddem's *Past Due* bill from Orsik & Arrbale. She would probably save that for last. It would make a good finale.

Chapter 2
DON'T FENCE ME IN!

Hermux set his tea and cookies down on the counter. He situated himself on his stool by the cash register and opened his new issue of the *Weekly Squeak*.

An article on page one caught his eye.

WHOSE MUSEUM IS IT, ANYWAY?

Donor seeks a room of her own

A Moozella Corkin Exclusive

Officials at the Pinchester Museum of Art and Science have delivered a surprising ultimatum to one of its biggest patrons – cosmetics tycoon Tucka Mertslin.

'We have asked Miss Mertslin to vacate our premises immediately,' explained museum director Dr Vannerly Parrunk. 'We hope that she will cooperate and that we can resolve this situation without resorting to force.'

The dispute revolves around Mertlin's 'unauthorized' use of one of the museum's most popular galleries – the Tucka Mertslin Gallery of Monumental Art. Named for its benefactor, the gallery was built to house the treasures of fabled cat king Ka-Narsh-Pah.

Problems began shortly after the gallery's opening last month.

'One day, without notice, Miss Mertslin simply moved into the gallery,' said Parrunk. 'She showed up with a moving van, cabinets and a desk. She ignored the guards and set up an office right in front of the king's mummy. The next thing we knew, she'd moved her secretary in too. Now she's got two secretaries. Last week she announced that the gallery would be closed to the public except for Tuesdays during her lunch hour. I'm the head of the museum, and I have to make an appointment just to visit her. It's a ridiculous situation!'

In an interview at her sleek corporate headquarters, Mertslin dismissed the museum's complaints as typical bureaucratic meddling.

'What is so ridiculous about my wanting a little privacy when I'm working?' Mertslin asked. 'After everything I've done for that museum, I can't believe they want to deny me such a small pleasure.'

Style guru Rink Firsheen agrees. 'Why shouldn't she use it? Have you seen her at that desk? She looks fabulous next to the gold mummy.' A longtime collaborator of Mertslin's, Firsheen designed the gallery space with her specifically in mind. 'I wanted to inspire her, and I succeeded. How can you blame her for wanting to spend time there? I can't believe they want to throw her out.'

Dr Parrunk outlined the museum's position. 'Miss Mertslin is certainly welcome to visit the gallery at any time during normal museum hours. But she must understand that she *gave* the gallery to the museum. It's not hers any more.'

'We'll see about that,' Mertslin countered. 'I'm not normally a very aggressive person, but once I put down roots, it's not easy for me to pull them up.'

Dr Parrunk has scheduled an emergency meeting of the museum's board of directors. 'If she is not out of the gallery by the end of the week,' he vowed, 'I intend to ask the board to begin formal eviction proceedings.'

'Just let them try,' said Mertslin. 'They'll find out that the justice system is not quite as blind as they think!'

Hermux finished the article. He tried to imagine anyone evicting Tucka Mertslin from any place. But he drew a complete blank. Just then the door opened, and a flying squirrel walked into the shop.

Chapter 3
SPECIAL DELIVERY

The flying squirrel pushed his goggles up on to his forehead, revealing a pair of very large round eyes. The squirrel stopped and appraised the details of Hermux and his shop. He saw Hermux in his orange plaid sweater and bow tie with his newspaper in paw. He registered the sales counter with its three heights to accommodate Hermux's customers, who came in a variety of sizes. The neat glass cases were filled with watches, and wooden shelves crowded with clocks lined the walls. The squirrel's dark eyes sparkled with a mix of curiosity and amusement.

'Hermux Tantamoq?' he asked.

'Yes,' answered Hermux. 'That's me.'

'Sign here,' the squirrel said. He was a messenger. He wore a brown leather cap with sculpted earflaps and a chin strap, a brown corduroy jacket zipped to the neck, matching corduroy trousers, brown boots that laced up almost to his knees and brown gloves. Over his shoulder he carried a canvas pouch. He slapped a clipboard down on the counter.

'Fourth line from the top,' he said, smoothing the fur along the line of his chin. 'And print your name below.'

'Goodness!' said Hermux. 'I've never got a note by messenger.'

'You haven't got it yet,' the messenger said coolly. 'What kind of place is this, anyway?'

'It's a watch shop.'

'So what do you watch?'

'I don't watch anything,' Hermux explained. 'I make watches. Actually, I mostly repair watches. Not many people get them made any more.'

'I had a watch once,' the messenger said. 'It broke.' He removed an envelope from his pouch, examined Hermux's signature, and handed the envelope to Hermux.

Hermux eagerly tore it open and read.

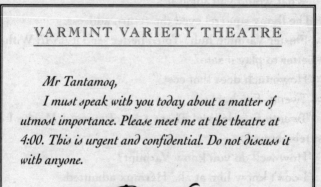

VARMINT VARIETY THEATRE

Mr Tantamoq,
I must speak with you today about a matter of utmost importance. Please meet me at the theatre at 4:00. This is urgent and confidential. Do not discuss it with anyone.

Fluster Varmint
Theatrical Impresario

P.S. Once you have read this note, please destroy it.

'Looks kind of serious!' commented the flying squirrel.

Hermux shielded the note from the squirrel's view and eyed him suspiciously. 'Just routine,' he said. He crumpled the note casually and slipped it into his pocket.

'So? Is there an answer?' the squirrel asked.

'An answer?'

'When people get a message, they usually write back.'

'Sorry,' said Hermux. 'I didn't think of that. You mean right now?'

'No time like the present.' The squirrel sounded a little bored with his work.

'Is that included?'

The squirrel shook his head. 'No. It'll cost you.'

'How much?' Hermux asked.

'Depends on when you want it to get there.'

'What would you suggest?'

The flying squirrel eyed the return address.

'Fluster Varmint, huh? You'd better send it *ASAP*. With VIPs it's better to play it safe.'

'How much does that cost?'

'Twenty-five bucks.'

'Twenty-five dollars! That's a lot of money! Maybe I could just telephone.'

'How well do you know Varmint?'

'I don't know him at all,' Hermux admitted.

'Then forget the phone. You'll never get through. It's the problem with VIPs. That's where I come in.' He pointed to the embroidered patch on his jacket. It showed a flying squirrel – arms, legs and tail outstretched against a brilliant blue sky. Encircling it was a motto:

'Guaranteed,' the messenger said.

Hermux thought it over. Twenty-five dollars was definitely

a lot of money. But it was exciting to get a note from Fluster Varmint – the most famous man in show business. Besides that, it was a mysterious note. And recently Hermux had developed a taste for mystery.

'All right!' he said. 'I'll do it!'

Hermux sat down and wrote out a note in his nicest handwriting.

> Dear Mr Varmint,
> I look forward to meeting you.
> Until then,
>   Hermux Tantamoq,
>   Watchmaker

He put the note in an envelope and copied out the address. He handed the note to the flying squirrel, who tucked it inside his pouch. Then Hermux opened his wallet and counted out twenty-five dollars.

The flying squirrel stuffed the money into his pocket.

'What's back there?' he asked, motioning towards the round doorway at the back of the shop.

'That's my workshop,' said Hermux. 'That's where I fix things. Watches and clocks. I'm a recognized expert in the repair of cuckoo clocks.'

'Interesting,' said the flying squirrel. But he didn't sound very interested, and he showed no signs of leaving.

After a minute Hermux asked, 'Hadn't you better be going if you're going to deliver that *ASAP*?'

The messenger took out a chewing stick and bit off the end.

'People usually tip,' he said.

'Tip?'

11

'Tip. You know — money! It's terrible when things get lost.'

'Oh,' said Hermux. Dutifully he took out his wallet again. 'How much?'

'Five dollars is customary.'

'Five dollars!' This was turning out to be an expensive mystery, and it had barely begun. Hermux removed a two- and a three-dollar bill and offered them to the squirrel.

'Both ways,' the squirrel said.

Hermux didn't understand.

The squirrel explained.

'Five dollars for delivering Varmint's message.' He stopped and spat a stick-chip on the floor for emphasis. 'And five dollars for picking up your message. Get it?'

'But you were already here for the pickup,' Hermux protested.

'Never mind!' the messenger said wearily. 'Give me the five dollars, and this time we'll call it even.'

Chapter 4
TEMPER FUGIT!

The Varmint Variety Theatre had once been in the very best part of Pinchester. But the best part of Pinchester had moved on while the theatre, which had been the site of Fluster Varmint's greatest triumphs, stayed where it was. The neighbourhood wasn't exactly run-down, but daylight didn't bring out its best qualities.

Not that it mattered that much. Most people came at night.

If Hermux hadn't been in such a rush, he would have enjoyed looking around. There was a big sale on used toasters at Gammelroy's Appliances. *Two for the price of one!* Which sounded to Hermux like a good bargain. There was a left-shoe-only store. And a discount fabric store whose windows were piled high with bolts of colourful cloth. The sign in the window said:

NUT PRINTS 50% OFF!!

But there was no time to linger. Hermux was in a hurry.

He rushed through the doors of the Varmint Variety Theatre,

barely pausing to appreciate the workmanship of their pumpkin-vine hinges and matching wrought-iron doorknobs. He was in such a hurry that he scooted right through the historic grove of artificial aspen trees with their hand-blown Spiffany glass leaves.

Crossing the lobby to the box office, Hermux scarcely gave the exquisite floor a glance. He remembered hearing his mother say that craftsmice had used more than a million kernels of corn to create its intricate pattern of fallen leaves. But Hermux was there on business. And he hated being late for an appointment.

The box office occupied a rustic hut that sat beside an authentic reproduction of a waterfall. It fell into a wishing pond complete with underwater lights and real plastic ferns. Over the years Hermux had made many a wish at the wishing pond. After his appointment with Fluster Varmint, he must remember to come back. It couldn't hurt to ask for a little extra help solving 'The Mysterious Case of the Varmint Theatre', which is what Hermux, thinking about it on the walk over, had decided to call Mr Varmint's confidential situation.

The box-office window gave off a cheery glow. Behind its window sat a hedgehog. As Hermux got closer, he could see that the hedgehog, who wore thick glasses perched on the end of his stubby nose, was adding up a long list of numbers on a cranky-looking adding machine. The hedgehog looked a little cranky himself.

'Mr Varmint?' asked Hermux.

'No. I'm Oaf, the bookkeeper. Varmint's inside. And I warn you, he's acting very oddly today.'

'My name is Hermux Tantamoq. I have an appointment to see Mr Varmint at four o'clock.'

'Good luck!' said the hedgehog. With considerable effort he pulled a length of paper tape from the adding machine and tore it off. He circled the total with a red pen. Then he grimaced and got to his feet. He stepped out of the box office and locked the door behind him.

'Follow me,' he told Hermux. 'And if he gets temperamental, I suggest you run. I'll be ahead of you.'

'How will I know if he's getting temperamental?' asked Hermux.

'You'll know! Believe me, you'll know!'

The hedgehog opened one of the thick padded doors that led into the theatre. Inside it was pitch-black. Hermux couldn't see a thing. The hedgehog grasped Hermux by the arm and dragged him forward into the dark auditorium.

'Varmint?' he called. 'Where are you?'

In the centre of the theatre, a small lamp came on, silhouetting two figures seated at a table. The table was littered with coffee cups, cheese bits and papers.

'You're late!' a voice boomed. 'The audition's closed! We're full up! If you're not on the schedule, you're out!'

'It's me, Oaf!' explained the hedgehog. 'I've got the box-office numbers from last night.'

'Well, why didn't you say so?' the voice asked. 'Let's see them! And stop sneaking up on me!'

'Dad!' a feminine voice objected. 'Calm down!'

'I *am* calm!'

'You are not calm.'

The hedgehog pulled Hermux towards the voices, feeling his way through a maze of tables and chairs. Backlit by the table lamp, Hermux could make out the figures of two mice. A man and a woman.

The hedgehog darted forward and handed the adding-machine tape to the man. Then, moving with great speed and agility, he dodged behind Hermux, apparently using Hermux as a shield.

'And there's a gentleman here to see you,' he said mildly.

'Out of the question!' the mouse said. He studied the tape under the light. 'I'm not seeing anyone! No agents! No salesmen! No fans! If you want to see me, make an appointment!'

'But I have an appointment,' Hermux tried to explain.

At that moment the curtain rose, revealing a brightly lit stage. In its centre, three white mice in dark glasses were struggling to roll a gigantic and very realistic-looking butcher knife into position. But the knife refused to budge. Its wheels seemed to be stuck.

'On the count of three!' the lead mouse said. 'One! Two! Three!' The mice threw their combined weight against the handle of the knife, and it lurched forward, gathering speed as it crossed the stage. The mice raced after it. But the huge blade shot past its mark and stabbed into the side curtain. There was a sound of ripping fabric and a crash as something heavy hit the floor backstage.

An ominous silence fell over the theatre.

'Could you give us a minute?' one of the mice pleaded. 'We're not quite ready.'

'You'll never be ready!' exploded Fluster Varmint. He shook his fist at the mice. 'Get off my stage before you destroy the whole theatre!'

A chipmunk dressed as a potato stepped out from the side of the stage.

'Should I dance now?' he asked plaintively.

'No!' blared Varmint. He was a barrel-chested mouse with a big baritone. It shook the theatre.

'Dad?' the woman said reasonably. 'Why don't we put the

juggling twins on next?'

'No!' Varmint ordered. 'No juggling. And no twins! I hate twins! In fact, I hate everything!' He leapt to his feet, knocking over his chair. 'Bring up the lights! The audition is over! All of you! Get out of here!'

Behind him Hermux felt the hedgehog moving towards the aisle. As the house lights came on, Hermux could see that the theatre held a goodly number of hopeful performers. Seated in the first row, a tiny, pale brown rat in a firefly costume began to sob. She gathered an armful of sheet music to her thin chest and then ran up the aisle, tears streaming down her face and pigtails flying behind her.

Her mother ran to catch up. 'We came all the way from Twyrp for this!' she moaned as she rushed by. 'And she's been practising for months!'

The aisle was jammed now with disappointed performers moving towards the exits. A noisy group of prairie-dog impersonators wearing matching paisley boleros, toreador trousers and very high, high heels pushed past Hermux and surrounded Varmint, barking at him furiously.

Varmint responded by plugging his ears and walking away.

When he reached the exit, he stopped, turned and waved to his daughter.

'Honey!' he yelled. 'I've got a splitting headache. Could you send me up a cup of coffee and some aspirin?' Then he disappeared.

The woman at the table nodded. She closed her notebook and calmly rose to her feet. She faced the prairie dogs and smiled sympathetically. Her smile revealed two perfect front teeth – long, elegantly arched and tinted a very pleasing pale yellow.

'Please forgive my father,' she asked the prairie dogs in a

17

genuinely warm tone of voice. 'He's not himself today. Perhaps you can come back next week. There are still some great openings in the *Silver Jubilee* show.'

That didn't quite seem to satisfy the prairie dogs, but after talking among themselves, they tottered away, grumbling about Varmint's lack of respect for artists of their stature.

The woman then turned to Hermux.

'I'm sorry, but I think the audition is over for today. If you give me your name, I'll schedule you for an early slot next week.'

'I'm not here for an audition,' Hermux told her politely. 'Mr Varmint asked to see me. My name is Hermux Tantamoq.'

'It's very nice to meet you, Mr Tantamoq. I'm Beulith Varmint, the theatre's manager and his daughter, as you've probably guessed. What did my father want to see you about?'

Hermux considered how to answer her. Mr Varmint had instructed Hermux not to speak to anyone about his note. Besides, Hermux didn't actually know why Varmint wanted to see him. He looked at Beulith. Her ears were enormous. Her eyes were wide set and lustrous. Above each eye and from each side of her long, tapered snout sprang thick tufts of dark whiskers that contrasted dramatically with her pale brown fur. Beulith Varmint was, in short, a very beautiful mouse. She also looked like a mouse who expected a truthful answer when she asked a question.

Hermux decided to be as honest as he could be under the circumstances.

'I'm not entirely sure why your father sent for me. Perhaps it has something to do with a clock.' He handed her a business card. 'I'm a watchmaker, you see.'

Chapter 5
MEMORIES ARE MADE OF THIS

'I'm home!' Hermux announced cheerily from the front door. 'And I've got lots to tell you! Are you awake?' He hung up his coat and scarf and went immediately to his study.

Terfle was not asleep. She wasn't even sleepy. She had timed her afternoon nap very carefully, allowing herself four full minutes for yawning, rubbing her eyes, opening her ruby-red elytra and stretching her delicate wings. She had wanted to be awake and alert when Hermux arrived home from the shop. She had been waiting for more than twelve minutes (and just starting to worry about him) when she heard his key in the door.

'How are you, little bug?' he asked, peering eagerly through the bars of her cage. 'You're looking very pretty. I'll get us a little fire started, and then I'm going to make us a special dinner.'

Hermux wanted the whole evening to be special. Especially for Terfle. This might be their last evening alone together for some time. Terfle was Hermux's pet ladybird. And although she was not usually a jealous or temperamental bug, Hermux couldn't help worrying that with Linka coming home tomorrow, Terfle might find herself feeling a bit neglected in the days to come.

'I've had a very interesting day,' Hermux explained as he

arranged newspaper and kindling in the fireplace. 'I received a message from a messenger. It's very expensive, you know.' He struck a match and lit the newspaper. 'It was from Fluster Varmint himself. It sounds like he's in trouble.' As the kindling caught fire, Hermux added small pieces of firewood. 'He told me to come to the theatre. And when I got there, he was having a rehearsal. But before I could speak to him, Mr Varmint started shouting at everyone and walked out with no explanation. I'm not sure what that means. He might be under a lot of pressure. Or he may be mentally unstable. Or both. What do you think?'

Terfle didn't know what to think. She would need more information before she could make a mental-health assessment on a total stranger.

'I think I've got this fire going,' Hermux said. He added a log to the flames. 'I'll change clothes and go make dinner. And then I'll be right back. Don't go away!'

When Hermux returned, he was carrying a large tray. On it sat a steaming bowl of sweet potato soup. Next to the bowl sat a much smaller tray. And on that tray sat a tiny saucer of jellied aphids. Hermux sat the big tray down by his easy chair. Then he carried the small tray to Terfle's cage. He opened the door and set it carefully inside.

'I think you'll like this,' he said. Terfle couldn't quite believe her eyes. Jellied aphids! And it wasn't even a holiday. She approached the saucer with as much dignity as she could muster, trying not to appear rushed or greedy. But at the last moment her resolve melted away. She leapt forward and buried her face in the pale green jelly.

'There's more, if you finish that,' Hermux told her.

Terfle responded with a faint, but somewhat unladylike, slurp.

After Hermux had finished his bowl of soup and Terfle had finished her third saucer of aphids, Hermux cleared away the dishes. Then he added another log to the fire and put on some music. He opened Terfle's cage and offered her his paw. She crawled up his arm and settled on his shoulder.

Before long, the excellent dinner, the warmth of the fire and the sweet strains of Todgerleakun's 'Duet for Cricket and Harp' conspired to make Terfle feel very sleepy. She snuggled down into the thick flannel of Hermux's robe and began to purr.

'Oh, no, you don't!' said Hermux. 'It's too early to go to bed. Besides, I have another surprise for you. I got a postcard today. From Linka. It has a photo of a volcano on it. Linka says to say hello to you.'

He showed Terfle the postcard.

'She should be home tomorrow,' he added hesitantly.

That was both good news and bad news to Terfle. The good news was that Linka always brought her an interesting gift when she returned from an adventure. This time Linka had promised to look for a small seashell that Terfle might use as a bathtub. The bad news was that Hermux would be busy again, spending all his free time with Linka. Terfle liked Linka. She really did. Linka was thoughtful, and she lived a very interesting life, travelling and having adventures. Maybe it wasn't fair to compare herself to Linka. 'But it's hard to feel very interesting,' she thought, 'when you spend all your time at home, alone in a cage.'

Terfle stared at the postcard but didn't respond. Maybe it was not going to be such a nice evening after all.

'I thought we could put it in our scrapbook,' suggested Hermux.

Working on their scrapbook was one of Terfle's favourite

things to do. She considered her options. She could have a good sulk, but there would be plenty of time for that during the long, lonely evenings ahead. She looked up at Hermux and waved her antennae.

'OK!' he said. 'Then let's get to work!'

Hermux placed Terfle on the perch that stood on his desk. He had made it for her especially for working on the scrapbook. From her perch she could see everything he did. Terfle had strong views on photographs and newspaper clippings. She liked them cut out with clean, straight edges. And she liked them pasted down neatly, without drips or crimps or lumps. She also liked to review all of their previous work before they got started. So Hermux got down the scrapbook, set it on the desk and opened it to page one.

At its centre was a repair tag from Hermux's watch shop. It described a woman's badly damaged wristwatch left for repair. The owner was Linka Perflinger of number 3 Pickdorndle Lane. She had never returned for it. Then one day a suspicious-acting rat appeared and demanded the watch. That marked the beginning of Hermux's very first adventure. The next pages included an article from the *Weekly Squeak* about a dangerous expedition to faraway Teulabonari, a photograph of a mole named Dr Mennus – a plastic surgeon with a sinister reputation – and a newspaper clipping that told how Hermux had rescued Linka from a creepy health spa named the Last Resort.

Hermux gave Terfle time to study each page before he turned to the next. Midway through the book was an invitation to Mirrin Stentrill's art show at the Pinchester Museum of Art and Science. And an article about the riot that happened there. That was the beginning of Hermux's second adventure. There was a photograph of Hermux and a chipmunk named Birch

Tentintrotter standing on the desert in front of Linka's plane. They were on a search for the tomb of the ancient cat king Ka-Narsh-Pah.

There was also a map to the king's tomb. It was written in hieroglyphics. And a ticket to a show on a showboat starring Tucka Mertslin. Then there was a newspaper story about her boyfriend, who was a famous man who had gone completely evil or totally insane and tried to kill Hermux and Linka and Birch. Finally there was an invitation to the Pinchester Museum to see the golden mummy of Ka-Narsh-Pah and his dancing-mouse clock that Hermux had helped find and repair. Terfle especially liked that adventure because it ended happily for their friend Mirrin. After many years of loneliness and waiting, Mirrin and Birch were reunited, and finally married.

The scrapbook brought back a lot of memories for Hermux and Terfle. It was a very pleasant way to spend an evening.

Hermux positioned Linka's postcard on a fresh page.

'Should I put it in the middle, like this?' he asked. 'Or more towards the top?'

Terfle preferred it lower on the page. And she didn't want it pasted in place. She wanted it taped along one side so it could be opened and read on the back. When that was done, they both stopped and admired it.

'It feels like time for a new adventure to get started,' said Hermux. He stifled a yawn. 'But right now, I guess it's time for both of us to get to bed.'

Hermux carried Terfle back to her cage and said goodnight. Then he brushed his teeth and his fur and got into bed. He opened his journal. He thought back over his day. Then he smiled as he wrote:

Thank you for postcards. And for messages personally delivered by messenger (despite the extra costs involved). Thank you for theatres. For aspen trees, corn-kernel mosaics and wishing ponds. Thank you for helpful hedgehogs and temperamental impresarios. Thank you for soup. For fireplaces. For scissors, paste and memories.

Chapter 6
THE RETURN OF THE WANDERER

The next morning, when Hermux arrived at Lanayda's Coffee Shop, he got a nice surprise. Hermux loved a good doughnut with his morning coffee, and Lanayda Prink made the best doughnuts in Pinchester. That morning, she was introducing her new celery doughnut. Hermux ordered one right away. He wasn't disappointed. It was extremely tasty, nutty and sweet. He could easily have eaten more than one.

It was a nice way to start the day. And it was already a beautiful day to start with – warm and sunny and breezy.

Mornings at Hermux's shop were often quiet. It was usually a good time for him to work in his workshop. Hermux decided to start with something easy – Bratchlin Weffup's wind-up alarm clock. For some reason the alarm bell had stopped ringing. Hermux suspected that Bratchlin, who was a very highly strung hamster, had a habit of overwinding his clocks. Hermux chose a small screwdriver and began to remove the back of the clock. As he unscrewed the first screw, he glanced up happily at the calendar. Linka would be home that afternoon.

The shop door opened. Hermux put down the alarm clock and set down the screwdriver. But before he could get up, a shortish mouse with reddish fur appeared in the doorway.

'Hi, Hermux!' the mouse said. 'I thought I'd find you back here!'

It was Nip Setchley. Nip was Hermux's oldest friend in the world. They had been friends since the fourth grade. Nip was an entrepreneur. A businessman. He loved businesses almost more than anything. And of all the businesses that Nip had been in, he liked the hospitality business the best. His most recent effort was a motel on wheels. It had six cars and six trailers, and it went everywhere. Nip had named it Nip's Rolling Hideaway. And since he had launched it more than two years earlier, he had devoted his entire life to making it a huge success.

Unfortunately, like all of Nip's businesses, it had failed.

Chapter 7
THE END OF THE ROAD

'The lemmings were the last straw,' Nip explained. He took a bite from one of the celery doughnuts that Hermux had ordered from Lanayda's. 'One cliff and the motel was a total loss. The worst drivers I ever saw. So here I am, starting over once more.'

'You'll think of something,' said Hermux. 'You always do. In the meantime, it's nice to have you home. Are you going to look for a job?'

Hermux tried to think if he had heard of any openings recently. But before anything came to mind, the shop door opened again.

It was the flying squirrel.

'Uh-oh!' thought Hermux. He had almost forgotten about Varmint.

'This needs a signature!' said the squirrel without bothering to say hello. He held out his clipboard.

Hermux signed and accepted an envelope. He recognized Varmint's bold scrawl.

The squirrel leaned heavily on the counter.

'Don't mind me,' he said irritably. 'I've got all day.'

Hermux tore open the envelope. Inside were two tickets.

And a note:

VARMINT VARIETY THEATRE

Dear Mr Tantamoq,

Here's two tickets for tonight. It should be safe to meet in my office during the show. Just act normal. If anybody asks, you're giving me an estimate for installing alarm clocks in all the dressing rooms. That might not be such a bad idea! Ha! Ha!

Until this evening,

Fluster Varmint
Theatrical Impresario

P.S. Destroy this note too.

Chapter 8
VITAL ATTRACTION

Hermux directed the taxi to number 3 Pickdorndle Lane. He asked the driver to wait. Then he opened the gate and walked up the walk. Before he rang the bell, he straightened his whiskers and fluffed out the fur on his ears. Then he quickly ran through what he was going to do when Linka opened the door.

'Hello, beautiful!' he would say in a husky but very natural voice. Then he would step forward, put his arms around her and kiss her right on the lips.

He took a deep breath. But before he could ring the bell, the door opened. And there was Linka in a freshly pressed parachute-silk jumpsuit that looked soft and clingy and rough and sturdy all at the same time.

To see her then, laughing and smiling, you would never know that she had got up at four o'clock that morning; piloted a small plane all day through stiff headwinds; unloaded cargo, camping gear and passengers; stowed her plane in its hangar; filled out her flight log, maintenance chart and expense report; opened and sorted all her mail; and washed, dried and folded her laundry before she took a well-earned bath and shampooed her fur from head to tail.

She took his breath away.

Hermux forgot to say 'Hello, beautiful!' All he could manage was 'Linka . . .'

'Hermux!' she said.

He forgot to step forward and put his arms around her.

'H-H-Hello!' he stammered. It was too late to kiss her. Instead, he extended one paw and handed her the bouquet he'd bought that afternoon at Thankton's Florist.

'I brought you these.'

Linka peeled back the waxy green paper.

'Clover!' she cried. 'How wonderful! I love clover!' She buried her face in the creamy white blossoms. 'Thank you!'

'There's a card,' he said, pointing shyly at a tiny envelope tied on with gold thread. 'And I have a surprise. I got us tickets to the theatre. To the Varmint Variety! It starts at eight o'clock.'

'Oh!' said Linka. She opened the envelope and read the card inside.

> *Dear Linka,*
> *I missed you terribly.*
> *Welcome home!*
> *Hermux*

'I missed you too, Hermux,' said Linka warmly.

They looked at each other for a long time, not saying a word. Linka's fur gave off the nicest smell. Hermux's left nostril twitched with pleasure. Linka closed her eyes.

He leaned forward.

She leaned forward.

Their noses were nearly touching. It seemed that his dream was about to come true.

Just then, the taxi gave a long, rude honk. Hermux's dream of romance evaporated. Disappointed, he checked his watch.

'I g-g-guess we'd better g-g-go,' he stammered.

'I'll put these flowers in water,' said Linka. 'And I'll get my coat.'

Chapter 9
BRIGHT LIGHTS, SMALL CITY

The marquee of the Varmint Variety Theatre bathed the entire neighbourhood in a buzz of white light. The bath helped. Bracken Street looked almost new again and nearly clean.

'How exciting!' Linka told Hermux as they joined the crowd in front of the theatre. 'I haven't been here in ages. What ever gave you the idea to buy tickets?'

'Mr Varmint is a new client of mine,' explained Hermux. 'He gave me the tickets.'

'What kind of client?' asked Linka.

Hermux hesitated. He certainly didn't want to tell Linka a lie, but he didn't want to violate Mr Varmint's confidence.

Luckily Linka didn't wait for his answer.

'Would you look at that!' she said suddenly. She pointed up at an enormous neon sign for Denteel's Perfect Popcorn. 'That must be brand new!'

The sign covered the entire side of a building. Gigantic kernels of popcorn popped from a glowing kettle. They exploded overhead like shooting stars against the night sky.

As they watched, a massive replica of Birkanny Denteel's unmistakably elegant paw swung into view. It held a saltshaker, and from the shaker sprinkled brilliant salt crystals that drifted down like fat snowflakes. Then a puff of fragrant steam belched from the kettle and wafted appetizingly through the cool spring air.

'Oh, my!' said Hermux, awestruck by the salt-and-butter vision of splendour.

At 7:30 the theatre doors opened, and Hermux and Linka moved forward with the jostling throng.

'This is such a beautiful building,' Linka remarked as they passed inside. 'Look at the ironwork on these doors.'

'It's a pumpkin-vine motif, and it's all handmade,' said Hermux. He was very proud that he knew that.

'I love pumpkins,' said Linka.

'Me too,' said Hermux happily.

The lobby was filling up with mice, rats, chipmunks, squirrels, moles, otters and others. They stood alone or mingled. They strolled in as couples. They chattered in groups. Everyone was dressed for a night on the town. They were expecting to have a good time. Fluster Varmint's *Lo-Life Revue* was the talk of Pinchester.

Varmint had had his finger on the pulse of entertainment for nearly twenty-five years. He hadn't always had a theatre of his own. He had started out small with a travelling show that played little towns and midsized cities. He only had a few acts to begin with. A comedian. A magician. A few actors. A singer or two. A tiny chorus line of dancers. But from the very beginning Fluster had had style. And an eye for talent.

It didn't take him long before he discovered his first star – Nurella Pinch – who went on to become a movie star and finally a legend of the silver screen. Then there was Furry and Findler. And Mootah Berlleen. And Toasti Chimerrink. He gave all of

33

them their first breaks in show business.

Then, twenty years ago, Varmint left the road behind. With his wife, Beulene, and his daughter, Beulith, he made a permanent home in Pinchester. He bought the old, historic Variety Theatre and renamed it the Varmint.

Fluster Varmint was a visionary. When he thought long tails were more elegant, showgirls grew longer tails. When he thought bushy tails were more provocative, they grew bushier tails. If Fluster thought hamsters made the funniest comedians, then suddenly everywhere hamsters were telling jokes and wearing peculiar hats. When he decided that chinchillas were the most exciting dancers, an entire generation of chinchillas bought tap shoes, moved north and settled in Pinchester.

Varmint was unquestionably the greatest showman of his time. He was restless. He was difficult. He was easily bored. He was always searching for the next big thing. And he usually found it, if he did say so himself. For instance, he claimed that he had single-handedly invented the intermission, the curtain call and the concession stand. His most recent achievement, and one of which he was justifiably proud – dinner theatre – was already widely imitated.

But Varmint wouldn't rest on his laurels. He couldn't. Audiences were as restless, difficult and easily bored as he was. He was working on a new concept he called 'reality theatre'. Sometimes the audience was in the show. And sometimes the show was in the audience. It was hard to tell them apart.

On opening night of the *Lo-Life Review*, a fistfight had broken out at a table full of gangsters. The fight was staged and the gangsters were phony, but a hamster and a gerbil still got seriously hurt. And that was only the beginning. There had been noisy lovers' quarrels with faces getting slapped. There had been bottles thrown from the balcony. There had been food fights. There had even been a false alarm for a fire, complete with firemen and a stampede for the doors. At every performance the audience could count on some sort of surprise. The problem was that not all of the surprises were pleasant. Ticket sales were up one day and down the next.

Fortunately for Varmint, that night the show was sold out. Perhaps it was because of the rumours. It was said by those in the know that Varmint was planning the most spectacular production he had ever attempted. Celebrating twenty-five years of theatre, the *Silver Jubilee Spectacular* would be the crowning glory of his career.

A brilliant career. One that had won him countless friends and admirers.

And more than a few enemies.

Chapter 10
BIRDS OF A FEATHER

Their seats were very good. They had a centre table on the third row in the orchestra section. All to themselves. Hermux was impressed. So was Linka.

'These are very nice seats,' she said. 'What sort of work are you doing for Mr Varmint? Are you building him a clock?'

Hermux responded by changing the subject. 'I want to hear all about your trip,' he said. He scooted his chair closer to hers. 'What are the Fanooshian Islands really like? And how did you like travelling with the Knilloquicks?'

'Oh!' Linka began. 'The islands! They're beautiful. And each one is so different. Different plants, different animals and different people. On Teenowak they have lizards practically as big as you or me. They come right up and – '

Hermux was distracted by a noisy argument at the table behind Linka. Two shabby-looking shrews faced each other angrily.

'You invited *me*!' the woman shouted. 'I ain't payin' for dinner! It ain't right!'

'And the way the lizards look at you,' Linka went on. 'It gives you the creeps!'

Hermux watched in amazement as the other shrew grabbed a fork and threatened to stab his date in the leg.

36

'You use a specially carved stick,' continued Linka. 'And you hit them right on the nose if they get too aggressive. Can you imagine? Mr Knilloquick bought every stick he could find.'

'I wouldn't mind having one myself right now,' said Hermux. 'How did he get so interested in sticks, anyway?'

Now it was Linka's turn to be distracted. Someone was waving at her from the aisle. It was a rugged-looking mouse. He wore threadbare jeans and a motorcycle jacket. He had a handsome, narrow face and extremely short, clipped whiskers. His ears were shaved. One of them was tattooed, and it looked like the other one was pierced with a ring.

The mouse waved again and smiled. Linka gave a small wave in return.

'Who's that?' asked Hermux.

'I don't know,' said Linka. 'I've never seen him before.'

The mouse with the earring turned away to speak to an usher. There was a crash in the balcony. There were sounds of broken glass followed by laughter.

'How did Mr Knilloquick get so interested in sticks?' Hermux repeated his question.

'Oh, he collects all kinds of things,' said Linka. 'What do you think he's doing now?'

'Mr Knilloquick?'

'No, that mouse near the aisle! He's pointing at us.'

Hermux saw the mouse hand the usher some money. The usher smiled and nodded. Then he stopped smiling and started down the row towards their table. He was a large usher. A marmot, from the looks of him. And from the look of his nose he was no stranger to fighting.

Hermux rose to meet him, but the usher turned instead to the table where the two shrews were still arguing.

'This table is reserved,' he told them. 'You'll have to move.'

'Too bad!' said the male shrew. He brandished the fork threateningly. 'We were here first, and we're having us a good time!'

The usher calmly took the shrew by the arm, twisted it behind his back, removed the fork from his grasp, set it neatly back on the table, hoisted him to his feet and dragged him away.

'Follow me,' he instructed the woman shrew. 'I've got a table for two near the bar.'

'Cute couple!' said Linka, smiling.

'Very,' said Hermux, trying to concentrate on her smile. 'Tell me some more about the trip.'

'Well, the most wonderful thing was on Tremillien. There were thousands of wild parakeets!'

'I love parakeets,' Hermux enthused.

There was some sort of commotion at the entrance to the auditorium.

'Me too!' Linka agreed. 'Every day at sunset, flocks and flocks of them flew out of the jungle.'

The ushers moved down the aisle, asking people to take their seats.

'They were brilliant colours!' remembered Linka.

All over the theatre, heads began to turn towards the centre aisle.

'Some were tangerine!' continued Linka.

Somebody important was making an entrance.

'And lemony yellow!'

People stood up to get a better look.

'And coppery green!'

Conversations died away.

'But I think my very favourite colour was this extraordinary

38

blue!' Linka reminisced. 'It's hard to describe.'

Through the doorway floated a startling apparition.

'It was a clear icy blue!' Linka rhapsodized.

A billowy cloud of colour drifted down the aisle, shifting its shape with each breath of air. It paused and changed directions, heading directly towards Hermux and Linka's table.

'In fact,' said Linka, 'it was the same blue as that!' She pointed at the approaching cloud. Her voice died away as she and Hermux found themselves enveloped in an impenetrable blue fog.

Then the fog parted and a face loomed into view.

A pair of dramatic dark eyes looked down at them. Voluptuous lips parted in a half-smile.

It was a hauntingly familiar face.

It was none other than Tucka Mertslin – the chairwoman and CEO of Tucka Mertslin Cosmetics and Hermux's next-door neighbour.

She proceeded past them to her table.

'How barbaric!' Linka whispered to Hermux. 'That's a full-length parakeet coat she's wearing. Do you have any idea how many birds had to die for that coat?'

'Quite a few, from the looks of it,' Hermux answered. Nothing that Tucka did really surprised him any more.

Tucka nodded curtly to Hermux and Linka and then ignored them entirely. Hermux Tantamoq was definitely her idea of low life. She waited for her companion Rink Firsheen, the famous designer, to join her.

'Thank you, dear,' she said as the handsome otter helped her out of her frothy blue coat. 'Say what you will, there's nothing like feathers for warmth.'

Chapter 11
MEET THE NEIGHBOURS

The lights in the theatre dimmed briefly. In the orchestra pit the string section began their tune-up, followed by the bassoons, the harmonicas and the glockenspiel. The audience began to quiet down.

The marmot was returning to seat someone at the table the shrews had vacated. It was the mouse who had waved at Linka. From a distance Hermux hadn't much liked the look of him. Up close he liked him even less. The little silver bell hanging from his ear tinkled as he walked.

'I hope you like your stick,' said Linka. 'I didn't see another one anything like it. Mr Knilloquick couldn't date it. Actually I think that he's a bit jealous that I got it.'

Hermux was only half listening. He was watching the mouse.

And the mouse was watching Linka.

'Not that he needs another stick, mind you. Between the two of them they must have brought back more than a hundred sticks. The plane was chock-full. Mr Knilloquick thinks they may have the most important stick collection on the eastern seaboard. Next week he's inviting Dr Parrunk from the museum to see them.'

Now the mouse moved so his seat was facing Linka.

'I wouldn't be a bit surprised if he made you an offer.'

'Who?' asked Hermux suspiciously. 'What kind of offer?'

'Mr Knilloquick. He may try to buy your stick.' Linka sounded as though it were obvious.

The mouse continued to stare at Linka.

'What stick?' asked Hermux abruptly.

'The stick I brought you. Mr Knilloquick may want it for his collection.'

The mouse twirled his tail in one hand and waved flirtatiously at Linka with the other.

Hermux frowned.

'Hermux!' Linka said sharply. 'I'm not suggesting that you sell it. If you don't want to, just say so politely.'

Hermux was about to explain that he was scowling at the mouse when someone tapped him on the shoulder. He jumped to his feet and turned, fur bristling.

It was Oaf, the box-office hedgehog.

'Mr Varmint is ready to see you now,' he told Hermux.

Chapter 12
THE CAN~CAN!

The hedgehog led Hermux down the main aisle, around the orchestra pit, through the velvet-curtained exit, up a small flight of stairs and through another door.

For the first time in his life Hermux was backstage. It was dark. It was crowded. And it was busy. He could hardly see a thing, but it was exciting just the same.

The hedgehog stopped suddenly. Hermux bumped into him as three chipmunks in overalls jostled past them.

'Watch out!' warned the first chipmunk.

'Coming through!' warned the second.

'Clear the way!' warned the third.

Hermux tried to take up as little space as possible, but some-one still stepped on his tail. Next to him stood a rat with a headset on. He was the stage manager. Before him on a tall, narrow, tilt-top desk lay a thick notebook. The pages were covered with notes written in four different colours of ink. The notes explained exactly what was supposed to happen at each moment of the show.

The rat spoke into his microphone.

'The stage is set and clear!' he said in a firm voice. 'One minute to curtain.'

Suddenly a door opened at the side of the stage, and a swarm of chorus squirrels in green sequined tights and tall, plumed headdresses burst forth. Squirming, giggling and gossiping, they made their way to their places.

Hermux and the hedgehog were cut off by a flurry of flying feet and swirling fur.

One of the squirrels tapped the hedgehog on the nose with the fluffy tip of her tail.

'Aren't you going to introduce us to your friend?' she asked. She batted her long red eyelashes playfully at Hermux. 'He's kind of cute for a mouse!'

Hermux blushed so hard that the roots of his whiskers ached.

'Sssssshhh!' the stage manager warned. 'Curtain going up!'

'Cue sound!' he said. Overhead a factory whistle blew.

'Cue music!' From the orchestra, a harmonica joined in the call. It was followed by the woodwinds. Then the strings.

'Cue curtain!' The curtain rose quickly.

'Cue set!' Somewhere an electric motor hummed.

'Lights! Come up slow!'

The outlines of a factory building appeared in the darkness. An enormous conveyor belt crossed the stage. Behind that were tall vats and more machinery and stacks of packing crates. It was a vegetable cannery. Even in Pinchester it wasn't the most likely setting for a musical number. Actually Varmint had built it for another show – a romantic melodrama called *The Princess and the Pea*. But it had gone horribly over budget and closed with bad reviews. The cannery alone had cost Varmint a fortune to build, and he was determined to get some use out of it.

That was when he had had the idea of the dancing asparagus.

A gasp of delight rose from the audience as the first glittering

43

spear of asparagus appeared on the conveyor belt. The squirrel was joined by another. And then another. One by one they rode the conveyor belt to its end and plunged from sight only to appear again moments later encased in silver cans that covered their torsos but left their arms and legs free to dance.

Moving in perfect formation, the cans marched the length and breadth of the stage. They turned. They tilted. And then they paraded up a ramp and stacked themselves four deep – shapely legs still kicking in unison.

The audience, including Hermux, went wild. He clapped until his hands were numb. When the curtain fell, he and the hedgehog barely escaped the stampede as the dancers raced into the wings and vanished back into their dressing room to change for their next number.

Another door opened and two field rats shuffled into view. One of them was dressed as a hobo, the other as a farmer's wife. She looked like a doll with wooden shoes and two bright yellow wool braids curled up on her head like snails. They pushed a cart of cream pies before them. They were squabbling irritably about something as they walked out on to the stage.

'What do they do?' Hermux asked the hedgehog.

'That's Furry and Findler, the comedians.'

'Gosh!' said Hermux. 'Are they going to throw those pies? I'd like to see that.'

'Yes, they're going to throw them. Very funny!' said Oaf gloomily. 'And they're going to make a huge mess. And somebody else will clean it up. Then they're going to argue and sulk in their dressing room until it's time for them to go on again. Ain't show business grand?'

The stage manager waved at Oaf and motioned him to come over.

'Wait here,' he told Hermux. 'More problems. I'll be right back.'

Hermux waited. While he waited, a little shrew appeared carrying a stand. A large leather glove was mounted on the top of the stand. And perched on the glove stood a bright green parrot. The parrot's eyes were closed, and it appeared unnaturally stiff and motionless.

Mounted on the front of the stand was a sign.

GILDEN BINTER
Ventriloquist Extraordinaire

& his terrific assistant

TERMIND
Parrot of 1,000 voices!

The shrew set down the stand. He checked his watch. He tightened his bow tie. Then he examined the parrot from head to toe. He slipped his hand into the glove on the stand. He wiggled one finger. The parrot opened its eyes. He wiggled another finger. The parrot turned its head. He wiggled another, and the parrot stretched and spread its wings. It looked very lifelike.

Hermux was impressed. He knew a thing or two about mechanical animals. He wanted to see more, but the shrew removed his hand from the glove. The parrot's eyes closed, and its body went limp.

The shrew checked his watch again and smiled a small, secretive smile. Then he reached into his jacket pocket. And he stopped smiling.

Onstage, pies were beginning to fly. But the shrew wasn't interested in flying pies. One by one he searched all his pockets, growing increasingly frantic.

'This can't be happening to me,' he muttered. 'Not now! Not tonight! Just when everything is going so well!'

The shrew stopped abruptly when he noticed that Hermux was watching him.

'It's my lucky coin,' he explained uneasily. 'I never perform without it.' He hurriedly checked his watch.

'I got to run back to the dressing room. Can you keep an eye on the dummy until I get back?'

'I'd be glad to,' said Hermux. 'What's its name?'

But the shrew was already gone. Hermux stepped closer to the parrot. He had never seen a ventriloquist's dummy up close. He wondered how the glove worked. 'It's ingenious!' he thought. He couldn't see any rods or wires. He was about to lean in close and look inside the glove when the parrot opened its eyes.

Hermux jerked back.

'Looking for something?' the parrot asked.

Hermux's heart stopped cold in his chest. Then it began to pound violently.

'Wh-Wh-What?' he said.

The parrot eyed Hermux with a glassy, cold stare.

'I asked if you were looking for something!'

'But you can't talk!' Hermux sputtered. 'You're a dummy!'

'Apparently not quite as dumb as I look!' said the parrot. Then the parrot closed its eyes again. Its stiff body perched motionless on the empty glove. Had Hermux imagined the whole thing?

As he carefully extended a forefinger towards the bird's head, a bony hand seized his neck from behind. Hermux yelped in pain and terror. He spun around.

'What are you doing?' demanded the shrew. His tiny eyes glowed an angry red. 'I asked you to watch my dummy, not touch it! Nobody touches Termind but me! Nobody!'

'I – I –' Hermux honestly didn't know what to say. He didn't even know what to think. 'I –' he started again. 'I was just curious,' he finally managed to say.

'Well, don't be so curious!' hissed the shrew. 'You've been warned!'

A burst of applause interrupted them. Furry and Findler were done.

When the curtain came down, the field mice in overalls rushed through again.

'Heads up!' they cried, pushing Hermux out of the way. This time they carried mops and brooms and dustpans. As they rushed about cleaning up the remnants of the pie fight, the hedgehog returned.

'Let's go,' he told Hermux. 'Varmint's expecting you now.'

Hermux extended his paw to the ventriloquist.

'It was nice meeting you, anyway,' he said.

The ventriloquist ignored him.

Oaf moved away, and Hermux followed. At the back of the stage was a set of stairs. They went right up. But Hermux couldn't resist pausing for one last look back at the ventriloquist and his dummy.

The shrew stood where they had left him. His head was bowed. In one hand he held what looked like a large coin. He rubbed it briskly, then brought it to his lips and kissed it.

Next to him the parrot sat motionless on its stand. Then it opened one eye. It looked right at Hermux. It nodded its head.

And it winked.

Chapter 13
ALL THAT GLITTERS

A short intermission followed Furry and Findler. As the house lights came up in the theatre, waiters dashed up and down the aisles with snacks and drinks.

Tucka Mertslin rose from her seat and raised one arm. In her gloved hand she held a glittering gold compact. She snapped it open with a practised hand. She activated its built-in vanity light and focused the surprisingly powerful rose-tinted beam on her own face.

'That should get their attention,' she thought.

In Tucka's other hand was an open tube of lipstick. It was unmarked except for a small handwritten label that read:

> **EXPERIMENTAL ONLY**
> *Batch #499301*

She brought the lipstick to her mouth and with a sure, steady hand she began to draw. Then she blotted her lips on a tissue and gazed at herself with genuine affection. Her mouth was a blaze of orange punctuated with bright pink polka dots. Tucka decided right then and there on the name for the new lipstick.

Dangerous

She threw her head back and laughed. Life was so much fun!

Tucka put away her compact and lipstick and scanned the theatre for people she knew. Two rows back sat Flurty Palin, the playboy, with socialites Skimpy Dormay and Birkanny Denteel. Birkanny, the oatmeal heiress, was gesturing at her menu. She was always trying to call attention to her paws.

'Yes, her paws are slim and elegant, and so what?' thought Tucka. 'I get so tired of these people.'

Spotting Moozella Corkin was considerably more satisfying. Unlike Tucka, Moozella did not stand out in a crowd. As a gossip columnist, Moozella had learned long ago that no matter how much she might like to, she should never outshine her subject matter. She should inspire neither envy nor pity in the celebrities whose lives she wrote about. Moozella surrounded herself with colourful people, but she herself wore only beige.

Tucka hated beige. But she loved Moozella. To be absolutely honest, what Tucka really loved was Moozella's column. And Tucka loved it best when she was featured in it. Tucka wanted a write-up for Dangerous in Moozella's column. Tomorrow would be perfect.

'Moozella!' she sang.

Tucka knew how to make herself heard. But Moozella paid no attention. She had turned her back and was lost in conversation with an extremely handsome mouse in a dark green tuxedo.

Tucka threaded her way among the tables. In moments she was at Moozella's side.

'Moozella dear, how are you?' Tucka cooed.

Moozella froze. She had been having such an enjoyable time

49

talking to the handsome mouse. He was new to town. And he was an excellent conversationalist. So curious about everyone and everything in Pinchester. And so willing to listen. Moozella had been more than happy to talk. It didn't hurt that he had distinguished streaks of grey in his dark fur that began at his temples and swept up to the tips of his ears. A strong, firm jawline beautifully accented his well-barbered goatee. Broad shoulders and a narrow waist set off a well-tailored tuxedo. He was the picture of worldly success. With a delicious whiff of mischief thrown in. Moozella found him irresistible. And the feeling seemed to be mutual. Their conversation had just taken a very interesting and suggestive turn when Tucka arrived.

Moozella recognized Tucka's voice instantly. It was not a welcome sound. Being a professional, Moozella managed a smile as she turned to greet her. However, despite her best efforts, a note of regret dampened the warmth of Moozella's welcome.

Tucka noticed it immediately.

'Oh! I'm terribly sorry,' she said, running her eyes over Moozella's attractive companion. He looked even better up close. 'I hope I'm not interrupting.'

As she spoke, Tucka stared boldly at the man. He stared back. It was like flint striking steel. The heat of the spark made Tucka forget all about polka-dotted lipstick. If only for a moment. Her hand fluttered nervously across her bosom, as though making an inventory of each one of the emeralds that hung there in heavy strands, and then it rose to fondle the enormous baroque pearls that dangled from her ears.

He watched intently. His eyes followed her hand eagerly from jewel to jewel to jewel. His perfect lips parted in a perfect smile.

'I don't believe we've met,' Tucka said with a perfect smile of her own. It stretched the bright pink polka dots of lipstick into shapely ovals.

'We've just been getting acquainted,' said Moozella. 'Tucka, this is Corpius Crounce. He's visiting Pinchester for the first time. Corpius, this is Tucka Mertslin.'

'Ah, yes! Tucka Mertslin,' he said in a smooth and resonant voice. 'I've heard people speak of you.'

'And what did they say?' asked Tucka. She raised her head slightly to show off her ruby-encrusted tiara.

'That you're very rich.'

'Oh, that!' said Tucka, fingering the diamond bracelet that sparkled conspicuously on her black-gloved paw. 'People do exaggerate, don't they?'

Chapter 14
FAN MAIL

Hermux hurried after the hedgehog. At the top of the stairs was a small landing and a door with a large gold star painted on it.

The hedgehog rapped sharply on the door.

'What?' a deep voice replied.

'Mr Tantamoq to see you,' the hedgehog announced. 'Per your request!' he added. He opened the door and pushed Hermux inside. 'Good luck!' he whispered as he closed the door.

In the middle of a messy office Varmint was seated at a messy desk. He rose and greeted Hermux noisily.

'Tantamoq! Come in! Come in! Let's not waste any more time. Sit down!'

He indicated an uncomfortable-looking folding chair.

'Make yourself comfortable,' he told Hermux.

The walls of Varmint's office were papered with posters, photos and show bills. A particularly dramatic poster on the wall behind his desk caught Hermux's eye: *The Varmint Follies, Featuring the Awesome Okey-Dokey Girls.* On it a line of shapely mice in ballgowns curtsied gracefully. Behind them a row of gentlemen mice in tailcoats doffed their top hats smartly and smiled.

'My first show,' said Varmint, noticing Hermux's interest.

'On the road for two years plus. A different town every night. Sold-out houses all the way! Now, that was entertainment! And what a cast! It was magic!'

Varmint turned to the poster. He pointed proudly at the second dancer. 'I married this one! Beulith's mother. Smartest thing I ever did.' His smile faded. 'We had some good times together.'

Hermux leaned forward to get a better look at her. Even from where he sat he could see the resemblance to Beulith. Large, elegant ears. Wide-set eyes.

'She's very pretty,' said Hermux.

'She *was*,' corrected Varmint. 'Beulene was more than pretty. She was a real partner and a good soul.' He nodded his head solemnly. Then his mood brightened. 'And look at this one!' He emphatically tapped the mouse in the green gown. She also had beautifully big ears. 'Nurella Pinch herself! The one and only!'

Hermux looked at the mouse in the green gown. Of course he knew the name Nurella Pinch. But he couldn't honestly say that he recognized her.

'I discovered her. My first big star!' bragged Varmint. 'Of course Nurella wasn't a star then. She was just my wife's best friend! Look at the two of them! So young and beautiful and innocent!'

And indeed they were.

'Too bad things turned out the way they did.' Varmint sighed and turned away from the poster. 'Bad things can happen to good people, Mr Tantamoq. That's the sad truth. And that's why I wanted to see you.'

He opened his desk drawer and from the jumble inside he withdrew a letter.

'This came in the mail three days ago.' He looked at the letter

53

with evident distaste. 'I'd like your professional opinion.' He handed it to Hermux.

On the outside it looked like a pretty ordinary letter. Addressed to Mr Fluster Varmint c/o The Varmint Variety Theatre. There was no return address, however. And the stamp and postmark were foreign.

Hermux opened it and removed a single sheet of thick, cream-coloured stationery, which he unfolded carefully.

Dear Fluster,

It has been such a long time. Much too long. We really must get together again soon. And when we do, I intend to teach you a lesson that you will never forget.

I hope you've enjoyed the intermission, because it will soon be curtains for you.

With malice aforethought,
a 'friend'

Hermux read it twice.

'Well?' asked Varmint.

'Do you have any idea who sent it?'

'Of course I don't know who sent it. If I knew that, I wouldn't be talking to you!'

'Have you received threatening letters before this?' Hermux asked.

'No. I may have got a few threatening reviews over the years.

54

And I've got my share of complaints, about tickets and seats and service. But I've never got anything like this. Nope. Never.'

Hermux recalled Varmint's behaviour at the rehearsal the day before. 'Do you have any enemies?' he asked.

'Of course I've got enemies! Don't be stupid! This is the theatre! The question is: Is one of them actually planning to kill me? And if so, which one? That's why I'm hiring you. You find them and stop them! I don't have time for it. Particularly now. I've got a *Silver Jubilee Spectacular* to produce.'

'Well,' Hermux began, 'it may not be as simple as that – '

'Of course it is!' Varmint interrupted. 'I've got it all figured out. You're coming to work here at the theatre. Tomorrow I'm going to announce to the cast and crew that you'll be installing a master alarm-clock system throughout the theatre. That'll give them something to think about. And it should give you an alibi for snooping around and talking to everybody. First, I want you to find out if this is an inside job. The postmark could be phony. And then I want to know if this is some sort of scare tactic to raise salaries around here. If that's it, there's going to be hell to pay! I can tell you that! You find out who the ringleaders are, and I'll take care of it from there.'

'And if somebody really does want to kill you?'

'Put them in jail, Tantamoq! That seems obvious to me!'

'It may seem obvious,' commented Hermux. 'But it may not be easy.'

'Not my problem,' said Varmint impatiently. 'You're the detective!'

'Actually, I'm a watchmaker.'

'That's not what I've read in the papers,' Varmint shot back. 'What about Dr Mennus? And Ka-Narsh-Pah? I think you may be underestimating yourself, Tantamoq. Listen! I've got an eye for talent. And an ear and a nose for it too. And you're the genuine article. So stop kidding yourself. I feel better already. It's like having a detective-in-residence and a full-time security guard rolled into one. I should have done this years ago. Now, let's talk money. What do you charge for detecting?'

'I don't know,' Hermux admitted. 'So far I haven't charged anything.'

'You may not be quite as smart as I thought,' mused Varmint.

There was a knock at the door. Varmint ignored it.

'Well, don't worry about the money,' Varmint said reassuringly. 'I'll come up with a fair price for you.'

There was another knock at the door.

'What?' screamed Varmint.

The door opened. It was the hedgehog. Behind him stood Rink Firsheen.

Chapter 15
SMOOTH OPERATOR

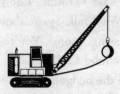

Rink slunk into the room with the liquid grace of an otter. He draped himself over a folding chair and threw his lush tail carelessly across several piles of theatre programmes. He wore his trademark leather trousers and slightly insolent grin.

'Fluster,' he drawled. 'How's the rat race? Oh! Excuse me. I meant the mouse race.' Rink looked pleased with himself as usual. And why shouldn't he be pleased? He was brilliant. He said so himself and most people agreed with him.

Hermux knew Rink's work only too well. Rink Firsheen and Tucka Mertslin had redesigned the lobby of Hermux's apartment building. First they had demolished it. They threw out the warm and cosy furniture. They threw out the chandelier and all the nice paintings of apples and pears and apricots. They stripped it bare. Then they hung up black plastic and barbed wire. And a bare light bulb. And they called it art.

Rink flashed his grin at Hermux.

'Ah! Tantamoq! Our little watchmaker!' he said with a wicked gleam in his eyes. 'What on earth are you doing here? Expanding your cultural horizons?'

Varmint gave Hermux a quick pleading look. Rink

immediately sensed that something interesting was going on.

'Don't tell me!' said Rink. 'You're considering a career on the stage! They blindfold you and you guess what time it is.'

An uncomfortable silence followed.

'Well, Hermux,' said Varmint, 'I don't want you to miss any more of the show. We'll talk again about your idea. An alarm clock in every dressing room! You're right! It could work wonders for the schedule! Oaf!'

'Yes?' answered the hedgehog.

'Take Mr Tantamoq back to his seat! And get Mr Firsheen and me some coffee. We've got scenery to discuss.'

Chapter 16
THREE'S A CROWD

When he got back to the table, Hermux was dismayed to discover that someone had taken his chair. He was even more dismayed to see who it was.

There next to Linka sat the shifty-looking mouse with the earring and motorcycle jacket. They were laughing. He threw his head back and showed all of his teeth and thumped the floor loudly with one of his motorcycle-booted feet. The little bell in his ear tinkled merrily.

'You're a very funny person,' he chortled. He raised his foamy mug from the table. 'To Linka Perflinger, woman of mystery and adventure! Hey! I like the sound of that!'

Hermux didn't. And he didn't like the look of it either. He didn't like any of it.

'Oh, Hermux!' said Linka when she saw that he had returned. She pointed to her companion. 'I want you to meet Brinx Lotelle!' she said. 'The *film* director.'

'The *action* film director,' Brinx said. 'Nobody likes films without action.'

'Brinx,' Linka continued, 'this is Hermux Tantamoq.'

'Oh, right,' said Brinx. He looked at Hermux without getting

59

up. 'You're the watchmaker. Not much action there, is there?' He winked at Linka. 'Why don't you join us, Hermux? There's plenty of room. Pull up a chair!'

'Don't be silly, Brinx!' Linka scolded. 'That's Hermux's chair you're sitting in.'

'You're right! Look at me! I'm horning in where I'm not wanted. But you can't blame me. I'm powerless when it comes to beautiful women!'

Brinx stood and offered Hermux the chair. Then he retrieved a chair from his own table and sat back down.

'The thing is, Hermux,' Brinx went on, 'I recognized the two of you when you came in. From the newspapers. And may I say, Linka, that you are much better-looking in person than in those lousy press pictures. Why can't they learn to take a decent photograph? It's a mystery to me. Anyway, where was I? Oh, right! I just wanted to introduce myself and say hello and tell Ms Perflinger here what a big fan of hers I am. Imagine meeting a real adventuress in this day and age! Now, that's action for you!'

'Brinx has been telling me about his next project. Wait until you hear, Hermux. It's so interesting.'

Hermux sat down and tried to look interested.

Brinx required no encouragement.

'I'm doing a documentary,' he said. He waited for Hermux's reaction.

Hermux nodded.

'A documentary!' Brinx repeated with more emphasis.

'What about?' Hermux asked.

'You're missing the point. I'm making a documentary. I'm an *action* film director. And I'm making a documentary! I'm making a statement. It's a big career move!'

Linka explained, 'He's making a documentary about Nurella Pinch, the movie actress. It's very romantic.'

'Mr Varmint was just talking about her,' said Hermux.

'Of course he was!' Brinx interjected. 'People will always talk about her. She was a star! The biggest of them all!'

'What happened to her, anyway?' asked Hermux.

'She had a tragic accident,' said Linka.

'Oh, right,' said Hermux. 'Now I remember. Pup Schoonagliffen showed me a newspaper clipping. It was Dr Mennus, wasn't it? She lost her fur.'

'It was ages ago,' said Linka. 'Then she disappeared. She was such a great actress. I must have seen *Little Mouse on the Prairie* a dozen times when I was young. She was so wonderful and brave in that. It's probably what made me decide to become an adventuress.'

'That's what stars do,' said Brinx. 'They change lives. They change the course of events! Nurella Pinch changed everyone who saw her!'

'Did you know her?' asked Hermux.

'Hermux, of course he did,' said Linka. 'They were married. Before her accident.' Linka turned to Brinx. 'I'm sorry things didn't work out between you.'

'Time heals all wounds. Even a broken heart,' Brinx said sadly. 'I forgave her a long time ago.'

'She must have really hurt you.' Linka reached for Brinx's hand and patted it impulsively. 'And you still care for her! So much that you want to make a film about her! It's noble, that's what it is. You're like an old-fashioned hero on a romantic quest!'

'Must follow the heart!' said Brinx.

'So where did she go?' Hermux asked abruptly.

'That's an excellent question!' Brinx raised his mug and

emptied it in one gulp. Then he wiped his mouth and motioned for Hermux and Linka to draw closer. 'Imagine one day you're the most beautiful woman in the world, and the next day you're a monster! It's no wonder she went crazy. Some people say she lives in an old castle in Grebbenland. She's never seen in daylight, and she stays up all night, watching her old films. Some people say she founded a nursing home for the blind. They're the only ones who can stand to be around her. Or that she threw herself under a trolley in Twyrp, and now she's buried there in an unmarked grave. They say that on moonlit nights she walks the cemetery, dressed in costume for one of her roles. Last month, it was the waitress from *Cheesy Rider*. The month before, it was Indigga Ooppincuff, the unhappy housewife in *Fur from Heaven*. Probably a hoax. But I'm going up there next week, just in case, to try to catch it on film.'

'So is she alive or not?' asked Hermux.

Brinx spoke in a dramatic whisper. 'The truth is – *no one really knows*!' As he said that, the candle on their table guttered and blew out. A bloodcurdling shriek filled the air.

It was Tucka Mertslin.

She stood up very slowly and put both paws in the air. Before her stood a stocky brown vole in a matching brown double-breasted suit. In one hand he held a gun. It was pointed directly at Tucka.

'Stay calm,' he told her roughly. 'Do what I tell you, and no one gets hurt!'

Chapter 17
GRAND THEFT

Waiters stopped in their tracks, trays aloft. Bartenders stopped their shaking and stirring. The entire audience was watching Tucka and the bandit.

'I suppose you want my jewels,' she taunted.

'Just put them in the satchel,' the bandit said. 'All of them!' He thrust a plastic shopping bag at her.

Tucka stared in amazement. First at the bandit, who was beginning to sweat. Then at the bag. Emblazoned across it in gold script was:

Your dollar goes further at Gammelroy's!

'First of all, this is *not* a satchel,' she said. 'It's a tacky plastic bag from a store I wouldn't be caught dead in.' Tucka knew she was stretching the truth a bit with that last statement. She did visit Gammelroy's from time to time if she had to buy a gift for an employee.

'Second,' she continued, 'I need both hands free.' She handed him back the bag. The gesture seemed to rattle him.

'Stay calm!' he told her roughly. 'Do what I tell you, and no one gets hurt!'

'You said that already!'

The vole licked his lips nervously. He looked so uncomfortable standing there that Hermux almost felt sorry for him. Hermux knew that facing Tucka would not be easy, even with a gun. He couldn't help wishing that the bandit had chosen an easier victim than Tucka. Hermux expected her to make a grab for the gun at any second. And if the gun went off in a struggle, any of them might be killed. Linka was the nearest. He looked at her protectively. He couldn't take a chance on that happening.

Then the bandit defused the situation by taking a different approach.

'Would you *please* give me your jewellery?' he pleaded.

'Certainly,' said Tucka. 'Now that you've asked politely.'

Tucka extended her arm, unfastened a dazzling bracelet, and flung it at him.

'A parting present from the Baron de Coude,' she sighed. 'It's hard to say goodbye!'

The befuddled bandit barely caught it in time.

Tucka rolled one of her long gloves down her arm. She pulled it off finger by finger. She twirled it once slowly over her head and let it fly. The glove drifted through the air and settled on the gunman's shoulder.

'Sapphires!' she sang. She slid the chunky ring from her finger. 'This was a gift from Marsupio D'Oligatini!'

It hit the bandit right on the nose.

'Ow!' he said, raising his gun hand protectively.

Tucka popped the pearl pendants from her ears. 'The Viscount gave me these! So many flawless memories strung together like these flawless pearls – the yachts, the parties, the casino, the moon shimmering on the Gulf of Tretch!'

She tossed the earrings at the bandit like peanuts.

'Stop it!' he whined.

But Tucka simply turned her back on him. A spotlight moved across the audience and focused on her. She reached up and unclasped the emerald necklace from her neck. She spun around slowly, raising the emerald strands to hide her face. She peeked through the veil of gems, moving her head from side to side and bumping her hips suggestively. She edged her way closer and closer to the bandit.

'Come and get it, big boy!' she taunted. 'If you're vole enough!'

Suddenly it was hard to tell who was the predator and who the prey.

The bandit was rooted, motionless on the spot.

'She's hypnotized him,' thought Hermux.

The situation was obviously spinning out of the bandit's control. His panicky eyes met Hermux's. The eyes of a cornered animal. His gun hand twitched, wavered and then dropped, helpless, to his side.

A wicked polka-dotted smile played lazily across her lips as Tucka shimmied closer and closer.

Then something inside the bandit snapped.

'Get back!' he shouted at Tucka. He raised the gun and aimed it desperately.

'I've got to do something before somebody gets hurt!' thought Hermux. He judged the distance between him and the gunman. He thought he could make it if he jumped as hard as he could. He lowered himself into a slight crouch, ready to spring. Linka tapped his arm lightly. She seemed to read his thoughts. A concerned look crossed her face. She shook her head no.

'She's right,' Hermux thought. 'I may get hurt. But it goes with the job!'

Then Tucka let out a cry of anguish.

'Not my tiara! No! It's too much! This was a gift from *me*! Isn't there anyone here who will help me?'

Hermux launched himself through the air. He landed squarely on the gunman's back.

'Ooof!' the gunman grunted. The gun flew out his hand. He staggered and crashed into Tucka's table. Then, bearing Hermux's full weight, he fell flat on his face. Tucka managed to save the ice bucket before the table collapsed.

As Hermux struggled triumphantly to his feet, Tucka lifted the magnum bottle of Fizzy Bitters 1992 from the bucket and clubbed him over the head with it.

'Tantamoq!' she said with disgust. 'You are a moron!'

Then she doused him with the bucket of icy water.

Chapter 18
FAUX PAW

The last thing Hermux saw before he hit the floor was an explosion of light. The last thing he heard was an explosion of noise. It sounded eerily like laughter. Uncontrolled laughter that seemed to come from everywhere at once.

That's what it was. Then, mercifully, everything went black.

The audience was still laughing minutes later when Hermux came to.

He found himself on the floor. His head ached. His fur was soaking wet. Linka cradled his head in her lap. Her warm paw rested lightly on his forehead.

'Are you OK?' she asked tenderly. 'You got quite a wallop.'

'I feel kind of dizzy,' he answered. 'Why is everyone laughing? What happened?'

'Tucka decked you with a bottle of Fizzy Bitters.'

'Why?' asked Hermux. 'I was trying to save her.'

'You spoiled her hold-up,' Linka explained.

'Her hold-up?'

'It was the Chef's Special. A De Luxe Armed Robbery served at your table with a black-and-white photo included. Tucka planned it.'

Hermux tried to sit up.

An ambulance crew pushed their way between the tables.

'I don't think I need a stretcher!' Hermux told them. 'I'm pretty sure I can walk.'

'I don't think it's for you,' Linka said as the stretcher was carried past them. 'It's for him.' She pointed.

Hermux was shocked to see the gunman being loaded with great care on to the stretcher.

'Where's Varmint?' the gunman yelled. 'I got a twisted neck, a sprained shoulder, a bruised arm and a sore elbow! I don't have to work under these conditions. Tell him I'm calling the union! Tell him I'm taking the week off! Tell him I want a raise!'

Then he saw Hermux. He pointed an accusing finger at him. 'Somebody arrest that mouse. He's insane!'

Chapter 19
CURTAIN CALL

Even Fluster Varmint was no match for Tucka Mertslin. Before he could say a single word, she interrupted him.

'Why do you let idiots like Tantamoq in here?' she raged. 'He hasn't the vaguest notion of the difference between fantasy and reality.'

'But Miss Mertslin – '

'Don't interrupt me! My evening is completely ruined!' Tucka turned away in tears. Rink Firsheen rejoined her and offered her his handkerchief.

'Thank you, Rink,' she said. She dabbed skilfully at the matted fur below her eyes while she sneaked a peek up at Skimpy's table. One glance was enough to confirm her worst fears. Flurty had tied a napkin across his face like a mask and was threatening Skimpy and Birkanny with a breadstick. Skimpy stood up melodramatically and surrendered a radish. At which they all giggled. When Tucka saw that, an uncontrollable screech of outrage burst from the depths of her soul.

'I want my money back!' she fumed.

'But you didn't pay for anything, dear,' Rink said soothingly. 'I did.'

'Then I want *your* money back!'

'Now, folks!' Varmint interjected. 'There's no need for all this talk about money – '

'Why not?' Tucka wanted to know.

'Yeah!' the gunman added from his stretcher. 'Why not? I'm suing you for on-the-job injury!'

'Excellent!' said Tucka. 'I think I'll sue for public humiliation!'

Then Rink joined in. 'I think I'll sue for missing all the fun!'

At that point, fortunately for everyone, Corpius Crounce stepped forward.

'Miss Mertslin,' he said suavely. 'That was a stunning performance. It's no wonder it was mistaken for the real thing.'

'Really?' she asked. 'You thought I was convincing?'

'Ravishingly!' Crounce told her. 'The world is your stage.'

Tucka liked the sound of that. She wanted to hear more.

Unluckily for Hermux, he didn't choose the best moment to interrupt. Hermux had diligently gathered up all of Tucka's jewellery from the floor and wanted to assure her that it was safe.

'Here's your jewellery,' he said helpfully. 'I think it's all here.'

Tucka swatted his hands away violently, sending the jewels flying.

'Get that worthless junk away from me, you nincompoop!' she ordered. 'I only bought it for tonight!'

Mercifully Varmint intervened. He raised his arms and asked for silence.

'Ladies and gentlemen! I think we owe these people a big hand for a marvellous performance!' He snapped his fingers, and a brilliant pink spotlight illuminated Tucka.

She knew right away that it was a good colour for her.

'Tucka Mertslin!' Varmint proclaimed. 'The one and only!'

A cheer went up. A drum roll rose from the orchestra pit.

Tucka accepted the applause without question. She stood regally, and then took a small, but very graceful, bow.

'Tustis Grivvin!' Varmint gestured towards the gunman. Hit by the spotlight, Tustis raised himself on one elbow and waved feebly from the stretcher.

'And finally, our newcomer, Hermux Tantamoq! Was he funny or what?'

'Yay, Hermux!' someone yelled from the balcony.

Hermux gave a half-hearted wave.

'Great show, everyone!' Varmint joined in the clapping. 'Wonderful! Really wonderful!' He slapped Hermux on the back. The impact made Hermux's head throb.

Then Varmint began herding people towards the bar.

'You're really gorgeous when you're angry,' Crounce told Tucka as they walked away. 'You do this wild thing with your eyes!'

'The eyes are the windows on the soul,' Tucka said, putting her paw on his arm. She looked up at him, arched her eyebrows and gave her whiskers a provocative quiver. 'In my case, as you can see, the lights are on. And I'm always home.'

'Then why don't I give you a lift?'

'My car is already waiting outside.'

'So is mine.'

'Mine is a limo.'

'Mine is a *stretch* limo.'

'Then let's make it yours,' said Tucka. 'I'm in an expansive state of mind.'

Hermux and Linka were left alone. Hermux sat down and let Linka examine the lump on his head. She rescued a piece of ice from the floor and wrapped it in a napkin.

'Hold this against your head,' she told him.

Beulith appeared with a glass of water and an aspirin for Hermux.

'Here,' she said. 'This should help. We go through a lot of aspirin around here. Now you see why they call Dad 'Mr Show Business'?'

'I'm afraid I made a mess of things.'

'Nonsense! Did you hear the audience? Those were great laughs. In fact, I wouldn't be surprised if Dad tried to make you a regular in the show.'

Hermux felt his head.

'I may not be cut out for show business.'

Chapter 20
WITNESS FOR THE PERSECUTION

The photograph of Hermux ran on the front page of the next morning's *Daily Sentinel*. It showed him dripping wet, sprawled on the floor of the Varmint Theatre. Over him stood Tucka Mertslin. She looked like a big-game hunter who had just downed a stag beetle with a single shot. She flashed a triumphant polka-dotted smile. The caption read: *Tucka Steals the Show!*

HI-JINKS AT THE LO-LIFE

by Moozella Corkin

It was a standing ovation for the Countess of Cool last night at Fluster Varmint's *Lo-Life Revue*. Looking positively Dangerous in her dotty new lipstick, Tucka Mertslin took the spotlight with a jewel of a performance. And in case you're

73

wondering, our Dynamic Diva still packs a punch! Just ask wannabe hero Hermux Tantamoq, who came between Tucka and the bandit of her dreams.

And speaking of dreaming, am I wrong or was that action film director Brinx Lotelle sipping Nutty Nectars with adventuress-at-large Linka Perflinger (just back from the Fanooshian Islands)? Is that romance, or a screen test brewing? Stay tuned.

Tucka Mertslin Cosmetics are available at Orsik & Arrbale.

Hermux threw the paper down in disgust.

'Romance?' he muttered. 'Screen test?'

Hermux sipped his coffee at Lanayda Prink's coffee shop as he considered writing a letter to the editor. Then he considered punching Brinx Lotelle in the nose.

Lanayda served him a second celery doughnut without even asking.

'Compliments of the chef,' she told him.

'Thanks,' he said.

'How's the head feel?'

'A little tender.'

'Would you mind signing it for me?' she asked.

'What?'

'Your picture,' Lanayda said. She handed him a copy that she had cut out. 'I'm going to tape it to the cash register. I like seeing my customers in print.'

'Me too,' said Hermux. 'But I prefer them conscious.'

Lanayda handed him a pen.

'Don't write over your face,' she said.

Chapter 21
LUNCH MEET

'Miss Mertslin!' trilled the maître d'. He bowed deeply. 'What a pleasure to see you!'

Tucka was a regular at the Swank and Swill.

'And may I say what a lovely surprise it was to see your photo in this morning's paper?'

'Yes, you may,' answered Tucka generously. She was in a very good mood. Tucka had decided to stop arguing with the museum and vacate her office in the gallery. Museums were such dull places after all. Besides, she had had a revelation. An entirely new vision of the beauty business. What she needed was more than an office. She needed a laboratory and teaching centre where her customers could learn the art of beauty by example – hers. They would see beauty in action throughout the course of a normal day in the fabulous life of Tucka Mertslin: Morning Beauty, Daytime Beauty, Afternoon Beauty, Evening Beauty and Late Night Beauty. And they could buy the products that made it possible.

Moving to a new space would require some sacrifices. But luckily they wouldn't be Tucka's.

'Mr Crounce is waiting for you,' the maître d' informed her.

'Your usual table, naturally!'

He led Tucka to the best table. It stood alone on a little island in the centre of the room. It was perfect for seeing and being seen.

Corpius Crounce watched Tucka approach. He turned his head away slightly, which seemed to emphasize the strength of his classic profile. Then he stood to greet her.

'You're even more beautiful than I remember!' he said smoothly.

'Likewise!' responded Tucka with an enigmatic smile. Her lips were painted in black and white stripes that echoed the black and white stripes of her power suit.

Crounce dismissed the maître d'and seated Tucka himself.

'So?' said Tucka, toying with the bracelet she wore. Like her outfit, it was striped. In alternating bands of white diamonds and black pearls. 'What brings a mouse like you to Pinchester?'

'A variety of things,' said Crounce. He couldn't help staring at Tucka's bracelet.

'Such as?'

'Business,' he said. He opened his menu.

'No time for pleasure?' asked Tucka.

'Pleasure?' Crounce gazed into Tucka's eyes. 'I've been so wrapped up in my work that I had forgotten about pleasure. At least until last night at the theatre, when I saw you standing there in the spotlight. There was such a glow about you. There was magic. Tucka, you're a star. You belong onstage for everyone to admire.'

Tucka beamed. She couldn't agree more.

'Of course, a woman like you is probably too busy for that. So, tell me about you. What are you working on now?' he asked.

'Right now?' asked Tucka. 'You! Isn't it obvious? I want to

77

know more about you.'

'Me?' Crounce laughed. 'There's nothing special to know.' Crounce stroked his goatee. 'You're certainly not shy, are you?'

'No. Do you prefer shy women?'

'Not at all.'

'How about rich women?' Tucka removed an enormous diamond earring. 'Excuse me, won't you? These are so heavy.' She cradled the earring in the palm of her hand, letting it catch the light. 'I love the sparkle of diamonds! Don't you? Real ones, at least!'

The diamonds danced in Crounce's eyes.

'You still haven't said what sort of business you're in.'

'Business?' asked Crounce, a bit startled. He sat up straight. 'Business? Oh, investments mostly. Right now I'm looking for something special.'

'I'm always interested in business. What sort of thing are you looking for?'

Crounce studied Tucka's face. 'Actually it's not a thing. It's a person.'

'That sounds intriguing. Someone special?'

'Very special. I'm looking for a partner for a special venture.'

'What kind of partner?'

'Someone I can trust. Someone with vision.'

'Someone with money?'

Crounce gave a hint of a smile. 'To be honest,' he said, 'it wouldn't hurt. Business is expensive.'

'Don't I know it!' said Tucka pointedly. 'What kind of venture?'

Crounce decided to play it boldly. He was having fun.

'Actually, I'm looking for more than a business partner. I'm looking for a partner in life.' He reached across the table and grasped Tucka's hands in his.

'I had almost given up,' he said, his voice laden with feeling. The next line was his favourite. 'And then by some miracle – I found you.'

This was music to Tucka's ears. Feelings that she had forgotten swept over her, and hopes that had been cast aside were kindled anew.

Crounce's eyes bored into hers as he stroked her wrist, using his exquisitely sensitive fingertips to monitor her pulse. It was racing. But then so was his.

Tucka savoured the moment. She took a deep breath.

'It must be our day for miracles,' she said. Her dark eyes smouldered with passion.

'Then you feel it too?' Crounce asked hopefully.

'I definitely feel it,' she said.

'Then we –' Crounce began.

'Before we start with the "we" business, I still have a few questions.'

'What do you want to know?' asked Crounce. 'My life is an open book.'

'Let's start with the investments. What? Where? And how much?'

'Oh, you know!' said Crounce dismissively. 'The usual. Stocks, bonds, real estate. All over the world. It's hard to keep track of the details. I concentrate on the big picture.'

'Of course you do,' said Tucka understandingly. 'And speaking of pictures, I have a small one I'd like to show you.' Tucka removed her hand from his and reached for her purse. 'You made such an impression on me last night that I couldn't resist doing a little checking up on you. And it's the oddest thing! I can't seem to find any record of anyone named Corpius

Crounce. Anywhere! What do you think of that?'

Crounce reached for his water glass. He took a long drink. He coughed. He cleared his voice.

'Not surprising really. I like to keep a low profile. I don't like to see my name in the papers. It's better for business.'

'I'm sure it is,' said Tucka. She took a piece of paper from her purse and unfolded it. 'And then I remembered this. A friend of mine sent it to me a few months ago as a friendly warning.'

Tucka spread the paper out on the table and smoothed it flat. On it was a photo of a mouse.

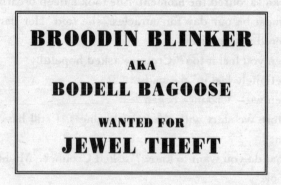

BROODIN BLINKER
AKA
BODELL BAGOOSE
WANTED FOR
JEWEL THEFT

'It's an interesting face, don't you think?' asked Tucka.

It wasn't really. It was a very average face with nondescript fur. It was neither handsome nor ugly. Nor memorable in any way except for a jagged scar above the mouse's right eye.

'Looks pretty ordinary to me,' said Crounce.

'But that's just it!' said Tucka with enthusiasm. 'It's unnaturally ordinary. Except for that scar. But look at this.' She took a handful of make-up pencils from her purse. She chose one that matched the mouse's fur colour and with a few deft strokes she erased the jagged scar. Then she chose a silver pencil and drew in streaks that began at his temples and rose dramatically to the tips of his ears. Then with a dark pencil she sketched in a beautifully barbered goatee. Finally she added a pair of stylish square eyeglasses.

'What do you think now?' she asked. She turned the picture around and pushed it across the table.

Crounce was looking at a portrait of himself.

Chapter 22
THE ODD COUPLE

'It's a good likeness, don't you think?' said Tucka. She took the poster back, folded it carefully and returned it to her purse.

'What do you intend to do?' asked Crounce.

'Do?' asked Tucka. 'Well, I've never been in a situation like this before. I suppose the right thing to do would be to –'

Just then the waiter arrived with their dishes.

Tucka smiled at Crounce and shook her head sympathetically. 'There's only one thing I can do, really.'

Crounce eyed the exit. 'And what would that be?' he asked.

'Why, celebrate, of course!' Tucka waved away the turnip broth. 'I won't be needing that,' she told the waiter. 'I'll have the quiche instead. Make it an extra-large portion. And bring us a bottle of Fizzy Bitters. We're celebrating!'

'Exactly what are we celebrating?' enquired Crounce as the waiter rushed away.

'Our partnership!' Tucka purred. 'Remember? Someone you can trust? Someone with vision? You know I can't stop thinking about last night. It must have been embarrassing for you to watch such a crude attempt at robbery. It would have been so exciting if it had been you. I'm sure I would have fainted. We probably would have got the whole front page this morning.'

The waiter popped the cork on the Fizzy Bitters. He filled two crystal goblets with the bubbly golden liquid.

'I propose a toast!' said Crounce. 'To the most beautiful, the most daring and the most dangerous woman I've ever met!'

'I'll drink to that!' said Tucka. They clinked their glasses merrily and drank. 'And I have a toast too. To you! The baddest boy of all!'

They drained their glasses. Crounce immediately refilled them.

'But I still have a question,' said Tucka with a wicked gleam in her eye.

'Yes?'

'Just how bad are you?'

'Very, very bad. Do you want proof?'

'That would be lovely,' said Tucka.

'Do you have something particular in mind?'

'Most definitely.'

'Whatever you want, my dear!'

'I want the Varmint Variety Theatre. I want it for my office. And I want it soon. I hate waiting.'

'You want the theatre?' Crounce asked. She amazed him. 'You want me to get it for you? A whole theatre? Just like that?'

'Is it too much to ask?' Tucka took a dainty bite of quiche. 'I did try to have an "anonymous purchaser" buy it for me. This morning. And for a fair price. But that fool Varmint won't sell! Isn't there something you can do to make him?'

'Nothing I can think of that's legal.'

'Oh! Legal!' scoffed Tucka. 'Who cares about legal?'

They both laughed.

'You get me that theatre,' she said, 'and you'll make me the happiest woman in the world. And when I'm happy, I can be very nice. I might even introduce you to some of my friends. Like Skimpy Dormay. She has entirely too much jewellery for her own good.'

Crounce thought he must be dreaming. He pinched his leg under the table. No. He was awake. After a lifetime of dreaming, he had found someone who liked him for who he was – a depraved scoundrel. And what did she want from him? She wanted him to ruin Fluster Varmint and take away his theatre.

It *was* a miracle!

He reached again for Tucka's paw. He stroked the silky fur on her knuckles. 'Nothing would give me greater pleasure than making your dreams come true!' he vowed. 'I'll get you everything you deserve and more!'

Tucka raised her glass and toasted, 'To my knight in shining armour!'

Chapter 23
SHARP CLAUSE

It was almost snack time when Hermux's friend Nip paid another visit to the shop. Hermux invited him to stay. He set out two orange-peel-and-carrot doughnuts and two pastries dipped in chocolate.

'So? What happened last night?' asked Nip. 'With Linka? And the theatre? And . . .' He glanced meaningfully at the lump on Hermux's head.

'It wasn't quite what I hoped,' answered Hermux. He opened a tin of Tawny & Tikkin tea bags and offered one to Nip. He didn't offer an explanation of the lump.

The front door bell jingled. It was the flying squirrel.

He had the contract from Fluster Varmint. It was twelve pages long.

'The return is prepaid,' the squirrel informed him. 'You'll be happy to hear it won't cost you a penny.'

Hermux started to read the contract.

'Provided I don't have to wait,' the squirrel added. 'Sign it, and I can take it right back.'

'But I haven't read it,' said Hermux.

The flying squirrel snatched the contract away from Hermux.

'Party of the first promises etcetera, etcetera, etcetera. Party of the second blah blah blah. And so forth. And so on. Nothing out of the ordinary here. It's totally standard! I see dozens of these every day. You're wasting time. Just sign it!'

Hermux signed.

The squirrel put out his hand.

'But you said it wouldn't cost me a penny!' Hermux complained.

'Delivery charges don't include legal counsel.'

Hermux opened the cash register and handed the squirrel five dollars.

'I'd keep an eye on the safety issues if I were you,' the flying squirrel advised as he walked out the door. 'That penalty clause is a killer!'

'What penalty clause?'

But the squirrel was gone.

Nip read the copy of the contract.

'That could be expensive!' he said, shaking his head.

'What could?'

'Did you know that while you're working at the theatre, you guarantee the personal safety of Varmint, plus his staff and all of his performers? If anything happens to any of them, you owe Mr Varmint ten thousand dollars.'

'Oh,' said Hermux.

'Plus damages,' added Nip. He continued to read. 'It must be a mistake.'

'It *is* a mistake,' said Hermux. 'Mine.'

'But he makes it sound like you're providing security services for the theatre. I thought you were just installing some alarm clocks.'

Hermux didn't say anything.

86

'Hermux? This is Nip. Your best friend. Remember? What's going on?'

So Hermux told him.

'If anything goes wrong, you're in big trouble!'

'I think I'm already in big trouble,' Hermux admitted.

'And how are you going to run the shop and do full-time detecting at the theatre?'

Hermux looked at the contract. He looked at his friend and smiled wistfully. 'You're going to help me?' he asked hopefully.

And that's how Nip got his next job.

Chapter 24
SUDDEN CHANGE IN PLANS

Late that afternoon, Hermux went to see Varmint at the theatre. He found Varmint and Beulith in the auditorium, going over the books with Oaf the hedgehog.

When Varmint saw Hermux, he shouted, 'Tantamoq! You're the mouse!' He jumped from his seat and raced up the aisle. He seized Hermux by both shoulders and shook him violently. 'You're the mouse!'

'I am?' Hermux's head throbbed from the shaking.

'Didn't you see the paper?'

'Yes,' said Hermux warily.

'We're sold out again tonight!'

'Is that good?'

'Good? It's wonderful. You're a hit! The audience loved you! They want to see you do it again!'

'Dad,' Beulith interrupted him. 'I don't think Hermux wants to do it again.'

'Why not?' asked Varmint.

'Well, for one thing,' Beulith said, 'it's dangerous! Look at his head.'

'That is quite a lump,' Varmint admitted. 'Maybe we could

use a fake bottle. What do you say, Hermux?'

Hermux changed the subject.

'I brought the sketches for your – you know – the alarm-clock system. And I need to talk to you about that penalty clause!'

'What alarm clocks?' asked Beulith, surprised. 'And what penalty clause?'

'It's nothing, honey,' Varmint told her. Then he turned back to Hermux. 'So, Hermux! The alarm clocks! Let's see what you've got.'

Hermux laid his sketches out on the table. The first was a drawing of a giant clock with wires running out from it in all directions. Then there were drawings of smaller clocks with more wires. And close-up drawings of a double alarm-clock bell. One seen from the top. One from the front. And one from the side.

Varmint bent over the drawings and scrutinized them closely.

'Interesting!' he said.

'The big clock goes in your office,' Hermux explained. He pointed to the wires. 'It's connected to all the small clocks and keeps the time synchronized throughout the theatre.'

'I see,' said Varmint. 'It looks very thorough.'

'I don't get it,' exclaimed Beulith. 'We're in the crunch for the *Silver Jubilee*, and you pick now to install an alarm-clock system? It doesn't make any sense!'

'Of course it makes sense!' insisted Varmint. 'Why would I be doing it if it didn't make sense?'

The doors at the back of the theatre opened with a bang. It was Rink Firsheen.

'Hello, everyone!' he roared. 'I'm here! Are you ready for this? I've got fabulous drawings for a fabulous set!'

Rink strode down the aisle. He tossed a roll of drawings on

89

the table. It covered Hermux's sketches completely.

'Am I interrupting anything?' Rink asked. He stopped and scratched the back of his neck with a powerful forepaw.

'We were just going over some ideas for new clocks for the theatre,' explained Varmint.

'If it's not Tantamoq again!' said Rink. 'You've become quite the little mouse of the theatre, haven't you?' He unrolled his drawings. 'These are just preliminary, of course,' Rink warned Varmint. 'Just to give you a feel for the direction I'm going.'

Varmint and Beulith pushed forward to see the drawings. Hermux tried to look too, but Rink raised his broad tail and blocked his view. 'Why don't you go run up a clock?' he whispered over his shoulder.

'Rink?' said Varmint uncertainly. 'This is the *Silver Jubilee Spectacular*? Right?'

'Right and right again! Questions?'

Hermux shifted Rink's tail to one side and peered at the drawings. A blue squiggle marked the centre of one. A pale gray line meandered across another.

'I think I was expecting something more ... more ... more ...' Varmint struggled for the word.

'More *spectacular*?' asked Rink. There was an icy edge in his voice.

'Exactly!' said Varmint. 'More spectacular!'

'Nothing says *more* like *less*!'

'And how much will all this *less* cost me?'

'In round figures?'

'Very round,' said Varmint wearily.

Rink opened a black leather daybook, scrawled a number, tore out the page and handed it to Varmint.

'This will get things started,' Rink said.

90

Varmint looked at the number.

'You've got more expensive, Rink.'

'Just one of the prices of fame!'

Varmint crossed through Rink's number and wrote down one of his own. He handed the page back to Rink.

Rink looked at the number. Then he added three zeroes to it.

'This is more like it.' He handed it back to Varmint.

Varmint crossed out two of the zeroes and returned it.

Rink barely looked at the figure. In very slow motion he crumpled the paper into a tiny ball. He opened his hand, and let it drop to the floor. He thumped it with his tail and it vanished.

'Looks like my schedule is filling up!' he said.

'But, Rink, you can't just walk out on us. We've got a show to do.'

'No,' said Rink huffily. '*You've* got a show to do. Good luck!' He rolled up his drawings and prepared to leave. 'Ah! What's this I see?' He laid a heavy paw on Hermux's sketch. 'How utterly charming! Drawings by none other than Hermux Tantamoq, watchmaker. And it's clocks. What a surprise!' Rink's face brightened suddenly. 'Fluster! If it's dirt-cheap design you want, why don't you hire Tantamoq here? I'm sure his set would keep perfect time!'

Then Rink stormed up the aisle and slammed the door behind him.

'Oh, Dad!' said Beulith. 'What are we going to do now? We were counting on Rink! It's too late to find somebody else!'

Varmint made an effort to pull himself together. 'Don't worry! I've still got a few tricks up my sleeve,' he assured her. 'So long, Mr Big-time Designer! We'll go to Plan B!'

'What's Plan B?' asked the hedgehog.

'I don't know yet,' said Varmint. He picked up one of Hermux's sketches. He turned it sideways. Then upside down. 'Hmmm,' he mumbled to himself. 'It might work.' Suddenly he slapped Hermux on the back. 'Tantamoq! What do you say to a career in show business?'

Hermux covered his head protectively. 'I don't think so,' he answered. 'But thank you.'

'Dad,' complained Beulith. 'Stay focused! Leave Hermux alone. He doesn't want to perform.'

'I'm not talking about performing,' said Varmint. 'Hermux can design our set! Rink was right. Look at these drawings!'

Beulith looked. 'All I see is alarm clocks,' she said dismally.

Oaf looked at the drawings. 'Me too!' he said.

Varmint sighed. 'Could I have some enthusiasm here? We're in a bind! It's time to think creatively! What do you say, Hermux?'

'I don't know how to design a set.'

'Tut! Tut! That's no excuse! If I only did what I knew how to do, I'd never do anything at all. You're hired!'

'But –' Hermux began.

'No buts!' Varmint broke in. 'You start on Monday!'

'Dad!' cried Beulith. 'This is crazy!'

'No, it's not, honey. It's theatre!'

Hermux spoke up. 'I don't mean to be disagreeable, Mr Varmint. But I can't do it.'

'You can!'

'I can't!'

'You're going to!'

'I am not!'

Varmint raised his hands. 'Don't say another word!' he said. 'Beulith? Oaf? Could you give me and Mr Tantamoq a few minutes alone?'

Beulith shrugged. 'You're the boss. I just hope you know what you're doing.'

When they were gone, Varmint grinned at Hermux. 'Relax!' he said. 'You need to think outside the clock!'

'What?' asked Hermux.

'You heard me! I'm offering you the chance of a lifetime, and all I'm getting from you is negativity.'

'I'm not being negative. I'm being honest.'

'Same thing!' countered Varmint. He eyed Hermux shrewdly. 'OK, I'll tell you what I'm going to do. You're worried about the penalty clause in your contract. We'll make a deal. You throw in the set design, and I'll forget all about the penalty clause. How does that sound?'

Hermux thought it over. 'Is there a penalty if I can't design the set?'

'No penalty. But you're not going to fail. Trust me. I'm never wrong!'

Hermux looked at his sketches again. He recalled Rink's faint and squiggly lines. 'All right!' he said. 'I'll do it. At least I'll try.'

'You're a forward thinker, Tantamoq. I like doing business with you.' Varmint lowered his voice. 'Incidentally, there's been an interesting development in the *case*.'

'What?' asked Hermux. He was all ears now. 'Another letter?'

'No. Somebody telephoned me this morning. They wouldn't say who it was. They want to buy the theatre.'

'What did you say?'

'No, of course. What would I do without a theatre?'

'What did they say to that?'

'They didn't say anything. They hung up.'

Chapter 25
FOOD FOR THOUGHT

Hermux gave his friend Mirrin's address to the taxi driver and settled back into the seat next to Linka.

'How does your head feel?' asked Linka. 'Has the swelling gone down?'

Hermux laughed. 'To tell the truth, I haven't had time to think about it. It was a busy day.' He gingerly touched the lump on his head. 'Ow!' he said.

'Scoot closer,' Linka told him. 'And turn towards me.' Linka rubbed her hands together briskly and then gently placed one of them on Hermux's head, cupping it lightly over the wound. 'It's called the "Healing Paw". My grandmother taught me. Now close your eyes and concentrate on the warmth of my hand. Let it take away the pain.'

Hermux did as he was told. As the taxi glided through the quiet streets of Pinchester, the warmth of Linka's paw erased all thoughts of pain from his mind.

'Quit smiling,' teased Linka. 'You're supposed to be hurt.'

'I *am* hurt!' insisted Hermux. 'Don't stop now. I could have a terrible relapse.'

'I think you're starting to show signs of improvement.' She

ruffled his fur. 'There. All better. So what do you think of the "Healing Paw"?'

'I think I'm going to need more treatment,' said Hermux. He wasn't kidding. He did feel a little strange. His head was buzzing. Hermux rolled down the window, leaned his head out and let the wind whistle through his whiskers and flatten his ears. 'What a beautiful evening for romance!' he said.

'What?' asked Linka. 'I can't hear you.'

Hermux pulled his head in. 'I said –'

The taxi screeched to a stop in front of a brightly lit house. The driver punched the meter. 'Here we are!' he said. 'That'll be three dollars and sixty-three cents!'

Hermux helped Linka from the cab and gave the driver a handful of money.

'Keep the change!' he said. He had always wanted to say that.

'Gee, thanks, buddy!' The driver tipped his hat and sped away.

'Hermux!' Linka said. 'Are you sure you're OK? That was a big tip!'

'Was it?' Hermux took Linka's arm and strolled up the walk towards Mirrin and Birch's front door, which was open. So were the windows. From inside came happy sounds of music, loud talk and laughter. And pleasant smells of hot food. 'Their place sure looks homey, doesn't it? So full of life and happiness!'

'Let's find you something to eat,' Linka suggested. 'You're acting a little light-headed.'

'That sounds good,' he said agreeably. Everything sounded good to him. Music, talk, laughter, food. And especially Linka's voice, even though it was hard to hear above the crowd.

Friday night was Mirrin and Birch's regular open house. All

of their friends had a standing invitation to drop in, eat dinner and stay as long as they wanted. That night it seemed like half of Pinchester had accepted the invitation.

Mirrin Stentrill was an artist. She was one of Pinchester's most respected painters and a very old friend of Hermux's. Birch Tentintrotter was an archaeologist and a scholar of ancient languages, including Ancient Cat and Old Mouse. After leading the expedition to find the lost tomb of the cat king Ka-Narsh-Pah, Birch had returned to Pinchester. He and Mirrin had married, and they had settled down to live in Mirrin's old house. Birch had been appointed director of the Institute for the Study of Ancient Cat. Mirrin had returned to her studio and had begun a new series of paintings.

Linka led Hermux straight for the buffet table. She parked him next to a platter heaped with sweet potato fries.

'You eat,' she told him. 'I'm going to look for Mirrin and Birch and tell them we're here.'

'Whatever you say,' Hermux answered. He took a handful of fries and began to munch. They were deliciously crispy. As he ate, he tried to focus his mind on the events of the day. After all, he was a professional mouse, and he had professional responsibilities. There were things he should be worrying about, including the mystery of Varmint's threatening letter and his own new career in show business. But Hermux simply didn't feel like worrying. He felt like eating another handful of fries. So he did. While he chewed, he remembered the warmth of Linka's paw resting on his head.

Mirrin interrupted his daydream.

'There you are!' she called to Hermux from the kitchen door. 'Linka told me you were here. Come help me a minute! And we can visit.'

Mirrin was grating sharp Cheddar cheese over a swede-and-rice casserole. When the timer on the stove went off, she handed Hermux two hot pads and instructed him to open the oven. Inside, Hermux found a tray of pine-nut popovers. Waves of toasty aroma radiated from row upon row of plump, golden pastries.

'Follow me,' Mirrin instructed. She threaded her way to the buffet table, warning people to mind the hot dishes coming through. Hermux set down his tray and barely managed to snatch a popover for himself before the hungry crowd closed in.

Mirrin pulled him down the hallway towards her studio.

'It'll be quieter in here,' she said. She closed the door behind them. 'It's been a madhouse all evening. It must be the nice weather.'

'Maybe that's it,' said Hermux. 'I feel pretty exuberant myself.'

He looked around the studio. There was always something interesting to see. Mirrin's working wall was covered with canvases. In front of it sat an old, paint-stained armchair. Next to that was an easel and two tables. One table was covered with cans of brushes, tubes of paint and a palette smeared with blobs of colour. On the other table was a vase of roses.

Hermux stood in front of the easel. He nibbled an edge of the piping-hot popover and looked at Mirrin's newest work.

'Roses,' said Mirrin. 'I know. I guess I am becoming a little old lady after all. But Birch got me started on them. So don't laugh!'

Hermux had no intention of laughing. He stared at the painting. One huge rose swirled across the canvas in waves of red and coral and pink. It made him a little dizzy. He sank down into the armchair.

'Are you feeling OK?' asked Mirrin.

Hermux looked up at her.

'I hit my head last night,' he said sheepishly. 'Or rather, Tucka Mertslin hit it for me.'

'Tucka!' retorted Mirrin. 'She hit you? Why?'

'It's a long story,' said Hermux. 'I'll tell you later.' He stared at the painting. 'It's very beautiful,' he said thoughtfully. He sat for a moment without speaking. 'How do you know if you're really in love?'

Mirrin regarded her young friend curiously.

'Love? That's a good question. I think love is a little different for everyone.'

'How did you know that you were in love with Birch? Did you know it right away?'

'Almost,' said Mirrin. 'I knew I liked him. Birch was full of ideas. He was smart and funny and intense. And he was so curious. He wanted to find out about everything in the world. I liked that.'

'Was he romantic?' Hermux asked earnestly.

'What does that mean?'

'I don't know exactly.'

'Do you mean did he serenade me by moonlight? Write poems to me? Send me flowers and candy and open doors and carry me over mud puddles?'

'I suppose so,' said Hermux. He sounded somewhat discouraged.

'No.'

'Really?' asked Hermux. 'Then what did he do?'

'He respected me. Birch respected me as a person. As an artist. It's not as common as you might think.'

'Oh.'

98

'And he put my happiness before his. That's downright rare.'

Hermux stared at the painting of the rose.

'Who are we talking about, Hermux? You and Linka?'

'Not me so much,' said Hermux. 'More Linka.'

'You mean you don't know if you love her?'

'No! I know that. Do you think she could love me?'

'She certainly seems to like you.'

'That's different.'

'Have you told her you love her?'

'Not exactly.'

'Well, you could start by telling her. And see what she says.'

'Maybe I could just write to her,' suggested Hermux.

'I think it would be better if you told her,' said Mirrin. 'It would be more personal.'

'What if I sent it by messenger? That's personal.'

'No, Hermux. Face-to-face.'

'I'm nervous!' Hermux said. 'I don't want to rush her.'

'You're not rushing her,' Mirrin said. 'Life is short. You can't wait forever. Linka won't wait forever. Things happen. Good and bad. Something could happen to you or to her. It's time to tell her that you love her.'

Hermux knew she was right. As he rose from the chair, an enormous feeling of relief swept over him. It was decided at last. He marched to the door.

'Wish me luck!' he said. Then he threw it open and stepped out into the party.

Hermux had no trouble finding Linka. She was standing next to the buffet table. She was talking to Brinx Lotelle.

Chapter 26
TÊTE~À~TÊTE

'See!' Brinx boasted. 'I'm even more romantic than you thought!' He wiggled his clipped whiskers flirtatiously. 'Well? What's your answer? It would make me very happy if you would say yes.'

'I don't know, Brinx.' Linka hesitated. 'It's so sudden. I can't just leave without explaining.'

'Explaining what?' asked Hermux.

'Hermux!' cried Linka. 'You gave me a start! I didn't see you there!'

'I just got here. I was talking to Mirrin. What's happening?'

Brinx reached calmly for the last pine-nut popover and popped it into his mouth.

'Maybe we should talk later,' he told Linka.

'No, please!' said Hermux. 'Talk now. Go ahead. Don't mind me.'

'Do you care, Brinx?' Linka asked. 'Do we need to keep it a secret?'

'Keep what a secret?' demanded Hermux.

'Tell him,' said Brinx. 'He's got to find out eventually.'

'Brinx has asked me to –' Linka paused.

'Asked you to what?'

'He's asked me to work with him on his documentary about Nurella Pinch! Isn't that wonderful? There's a lot of travel involved, and he needs a good pilot.'

'A pilot!' said Hermux with relief.

'It's not *just* a documentary!' Brinx chimed in. 'It's bigger than that. Much bigger! It's a Brinx Lotelle film!'

'Brinx is going to interview all the people who have worked with Nurella,' added Linka. 'The actors. The crews. Everyone who really knew her. We'll visit the film studios in Woodland. And her childhood home in Dranton.'

'Nurella Pinch was the greatest star of them all!' Brinx rhapsodized. 'The greatest! And we're going to tell her story. The story of the woman behind the star! The woman who had it all and then lost it. The woman who broke my heart! The woman who . . .' Brinx stopped. He covered his eyes with his paws and sobbed.

'It's all right, Brinx,' Linka reassured him. 'Let it out. You'll feel better.'

Brinx wiped his eyes and blew his nose. 'And if we bring it in on schedule, it's a sure thing for Best Picture. And I'll get Best Director too!'

'The filming should take us about two weeks,' Linka told Hermux.

'Two weeks?' repeated Hermux.

Linka nodded. 'We start tomorrow in Twyrp. There's a big Nurella Pinch Fan Club conference there.'

'Tomorrow?' Hermux was shocked.

'We have to move fast,' said Brinx. 'Time stops for no mouse!'

'I know,' said Hermux.

'We're leaving first thing in the morning,' said Linka.

'That's so soon,' said Hermux.

'I know. I'm sorry,' Linka apologized. 'But I've got to get home right now so I can pack and get things organized. You don't mind, do you?'

Hermux did mind. But Linka was an aviatrix. She had a job to do. And it was her job to fly people where they wanted to go. Regardless of whether Hermux liked them or not.

What he wanted to say to her would have to wait until she got back.

Chapter 27
CLASS REUNION

An abandoned car lurched against the kerb. Its windshield had been smashed and someone had built a fire in the backseat. On the building's porch sat two rusty lawn chairs. On one of them sat an old chipmunk in a dirty bathrobe and slippers. In one thin paw she held a cigarette. In the other an open tin can.

She watched with some interest as a well-dressed mouse made his way down the pavement towards her. When he reached her building, he stopped. He looked for the address. Of the four brass numbers that had once been over the front door, two had been stolen and never replaced.

'Is this 1209 Dead End Drive?' he asked. He had a nice smile.

The chipmunk took a drag from her cigarette. She coughed. Then she spat in her can.

'Your lucky day!' she wheezed.

He started up the steps.

She patted the chair next to her. 'Have a seat, dearie! But I warn you, you're wasting your time here. Ain't nobody buying insurance!'

He ignored her offer. 'But thanks for the tip!' he said. He

stepped past her, pushed open the door and went inside. On one side of a dark, narrow hallway was an even darker and narrower staircase. On the opposite wall above a battered trash can was a clump of mismatched buzzers. The well-dressed mouse examined them one by one. Next to the bottom buzzer was taped a new business card.

GILDEN BINTER
Ventriloquist Extraordinaire

The mouse smiled. Not such a nice smile this time.

'Well, Gilden, I hope you haven't forgotten your old friend.'

He mounted the stairs quietly. He found the fifth-floor hallway deserted like all the others. A bicycle was chained to the radiator next to the stairs.

The mouse stopped for a moment. Even though he was in excellent condition, the climb had left him panting slightly. He took a deep breath and then tiptoed to the end of the hallway. He stopped at the door on the right. He put his ear to it. Inside it was silent.

He knocked.

He knocked again, louder.

'Who is it?' a groggy voice snuffled. 'What do you want?'

There were footsteps. An eye appeared at the peephole in the door.

The mouse stepped back a step. He waved at the peephole.

'It's me, Gilden. Your old friend.'

'I haven't got any friends.'

'Sure you do, Gilden! It's me. Your old friend ...' The mouse stopped. He couldn't remember what name he had been using when he last saw Gilden.

He closed his eyes and thought hard. 'Was it Anklin Albatrots? No. How about Aggio Artique? No. It wasn't a double-letter name at all. Those came later. Was it Magner? That sounds right. But what was my last name?'

'My old friend who?' The voice sounded suspicious.

'Your old friend Magner. Magner –'

There was the sound of a lock turning. The throw of a dead bolt. The rattle of a chain. The door opened a crack.

'Magner Wooliun?'

'Exactly!' The mouse snapped his fingers. 'The one and only!'

The door opened another crack. A narrow snout poked out.

'Magner Wooliun! Why you old – Wait a minute! I thought you were dead! The blonde with the diamonds. She shot you. They found the body.'

'They found *a* body.'

'Wow!' The door swung open. The ventriloquist, bone skinny in threadbare pyjamas, stood there scratching his head. 'Magner Wooliun! Wow!' he repeated. He took in the mouse's expensive suit and his sleek fur with its elegant streaks. 'You look like you're in the money. So, what are you doing here?'

'Just passing through Pinchester. I caught your act at the Varmint Theatre. I was very impressed. Thought I'd pay my respects.'

'Wow! You really liked the act?'

'I'm your biggest fan.'

105

'Gosh! Thanks! Coming from you, that means a lot.'

'So, are you going to invite me in?' the mouse asked.

'Oh, right!' the shrew said. 'Of course! Come in! Make yourself at home. I'll put on some coffee.'

The ventriloquist's kitchen was dark and stuffy. A small window opened out on to an air shaft. Pots and pans and half-empty cans covered the stove and the table. The shrew lit a flame under the coffee pot. He rummaged through the dishes until he found two cups. He emptied them out over the sink.

'Let's sit in the living room,' he told the mouse. 'We'll be more comfortable.'

The shrew led the way into the adjoining room, padding along with skinny bare feet. His unkempt claws clicked noisily on the linoleum.

'Have a seat,' he said. He indicated the couch. It was covered with shrew fur.

The mouse chose a straight-backed wooden chair instead. He brushed off the seat before he sat down.

'This is good,' he said. 'I like a lot of back support.'

'Right,' said the shrew. 'I'll get the coffee.'

'How long have you been here?' the mouse asked.

'About three months. Getting in Varmint's show was a big break for me.'

'Yeah! He's the big man!'

The mouse examined the living room with some interest. The coffee table was littered with dirty ashtrays and back issues of *Modern Ventriloquist*. He picked one up and thumbed through it, skimming the titles of the articles: 'The Emerging Role of Ventriloquism in Modern Politics', 'Great Ventriloquists of the Twentieth Century' and a report on an investigation into fraud in the ventriloquism industry.

'So, when did you learn ventriloquism?' the mouse asked.

'Vocational rehab. I was doing four years for breaking and entering. It helped pass the time.'

'You were always the bright one,' said the mouse, rolling his eyes. 'Say, what's in the corner?'

The shrew appeared suddenly with the coffee.

'What corner?' he asked. He planted himself in front of a bulky object covered with an old bedspread.

'The one behind you,' said the mouse.

The shrew looked over his shoulder. 'Oh, that! It's nothing.'

'It's kind of big for nothing.'

'So, what are your plans in Pinchester?' The shrew offered him the sugar bowl. 'Do you take sugar?'

'No, thanks!' said the mouse. He got up and crossed the room. 'You don't mind, do you?' He yanked at the bedspread. It fell to the floor, revealing an enormous birdcage.

Inside the cage sat the parrot. He glared at the mouse.

'What are you gaping at, mouse-breath?'

The shrew leapt across the room and rapped viciously on the parrot's cage.

'You keep your mouth shut!' he snapped. He retrieved the bedspread from the floor and draped it over the cage again. Then he returned to the couch and fumbled nervously with his coffee cup.

'I'm shocked!' the mouse said.

The shrew watched him warily.

'So your whole act is a fake! The parrot is real!'

The shrew's gaunt face fell. His thin lips began to tremble.

'A total con!' the mouse went on. 'The dummy does all the work! Just imagine! Then who writes the jokes?'

'Who do you think?' the parrot squawked from behind the bedspread.

'Shut up!' The shrew's hand shook. He splashed coffee down his pyjamas.

'A scam like that!' the mouse said.

'All right!' complained the shrew. 'I get the point!'

'I don't think you do. I didn't think you had it in you.'

'You mean you approve?' The shrew's eyes lit up.

'Approve? I think it's brilliant! Does Varmint know?'

'Of course he doesn't!' The shrew drew himself up with pride. 'Nobody knows!'

The mouse nodded. He smiled his nice smile.

'What's Varmint paying you?'

'Look around you!' the shrew said.

'He was always a cheapskate!'

'You know him?'

'Varmint and I go way back.' The mouse took a clean white handkerchief from his pocket and meticulously wiped the rim of his coffee cup. He took a sip. 'How would you like to make some real money?'

'You workin' on something big?' The shrew was very interested.

The mouse jerked his thumb towards the parrot's cage and shook his head in warning. 'Why don't we go in the kitchen, where we can talk in private.'

The two went back into the kitchen and were so caught up in their conversation that they didn't notice a corner of the bedspread being pulled back from the bars of the parrot's cage. And it didn't occur to either of them that Termind the talking parrot could also read lips.

Chapter 28

OPEN~DOOR POLICY

Hermux stared at the calendar above his workbench. He sighed and turned back to the skeleton clock he had disassembled. He put down his pliers and sighed again. It didn't help.

'I could have told her in the taxi on the way home. I could have told her on the porch when we said goodnight. I could have told her at Mirrin's, right there in front of Brinx! But I didn't say a word! I just stood there like a polite little mouse and tried to smile while she told me she was going away for two weeks with Mr Romantic Filmmaker.'

He looked up at the calendar again. Two weeks away, a new date was circled in red.

The bell on the front door jingled. It was Nip. 'We're in luck!' he cried. 'I got a half-dozen celery. Fresh and hot! And I brought us coffee too!'

'Great,' said Hermux dully.

Nip spread out the midmorning feast.

'So far I like the watchmaking business,' he said. 'It's not bad at all. Are you still brooding about Linka?'

'I'm not brooding,' said Hermux. 'I'm just disappointed in myself. It's hard to discover that I'm a coward.'

'I don't know if I'd call you a coward,' said Nip, nibbling.

'Didn't you save Linka's life from Dr Mennus?'

'Yes.'

'And didn't you fight a giant scorpion for her?'

'I suppose so.'

'And didn't you rescue her from a roomful of dynamite?'

'That was more of a team effort,' Hermux said modestly. 'She cut the ropes.'

'Still. It wasn't an act of cowardice.'

'No,' Hermux admitted. He shook his head. 'I don't know what's wrong with me now.'

'Well, what are you afraid of?'

Hermux took a bite of doughnut. He washed it down with coffee.

'I'm afraid she'll laugh at me,' he said.

'Oh,' said Nip. 'There's always that risk, isn't there?'

'Yes. There is. And I don't like it.'

'But you have to take it!' Nip told him earnestly.

'That's easy for you to say. Did you ever tell anyone you loved them?'

Nip thought. 'Nope. I've never been in love.'

'Then spare me the advice.'

'OK! OK! I was just trying to help.'

'I know,' said Hermux. 'I'm sorry.'

'It's all right,' Nip said. 'You're lucky to be in love. I'd like to fall in love too, but I've never met the right person. You know, you never have told me how you met Linka.'

'It was pretty simple, really,' said Hermux. 'One day I was sitting here working, and suddenly with no warning at all the front door opened, and she just walked into the shop.'

He and Nip both turned to look at the front door.

At that exact moment the door opened. And in walked Beulith Varmint.

110

Chapter 29
WORKING ARRANGEMENTS

Hermux and Nip looked at Beulith without saying a word.

'Is something wrong?' she asked.

'Excuse us,' Hermux said. 'We were just talking about how the door could open at any moment and a remarkable person could walk in. And then the door opened and in you came.'

'I see,' said Beulith. 'I hope that's a compliment!' She smoothed back the beige fur on her cheeks.

'It certainly is,' Nip chimed in. He extended his paw graciously and introduced himself. He tried not to stare at her sparkling black eyes or the sweep of her wonderfully big ears.

'Nip is my oldest friend in the world,' Hermux explained. 'And my new assistant. Actually, Nip is an entrepreneur. He's just helping me out until he figures out his next move.'

'I'm very pleased to meet you,' Beulith told him. 'I'm Beulith Varmint. I manage my father's theatre. Has Hermux told you that we've hired him to design our next show?'

'No!' answered Nip. He elbowed Hermux. 'The sly devil.'

'Really?' said Beulith. She sounded concerned. 'It's a very important assignment, Mr Tantamoq. I would have thought you'd tell your assistant.'

'I was waiting until our regular business meeting,' Hermux explained. He shot Nip a warning look.

Beulith surveyed the coffee cups and the remains of the doughnuts.

'And which meeting is this?' she asked.

'Oh, this is just an informal get-together,' said Hermux. 'What can I do for you?'

'I brought the new contract,' said Beulith. 'But before I give it to you to sign, I need to have a serious talk with you.'

'Fire away!' insisted Nip with gusto. 'Whatever the issues are, I'm sure we can work them out. Here at Hermux Tantamoq, Watchmaker, the customer is always right! Especially you!' He smiled at Beulith.

Beulith smiled back. 'This is serious, Mr Setchley.'

'I can be serious,' said Nip. He stopped smiling. 'And please call me Nip.'

'All right, Nip. I hope you won't take offence. But I have to be honest with you. I'm not comfortable with the idea of Hermux designing the set for the *Silver Jubilee Spectacular*. You may as well know that I tried to talk Dad out of it, but there's no changing his mind. It's a very important show, Hermux. If you fail, it will be a disaster for us.'

Nip answered impetuously, 'There's no need for you to worry! Hermux has never let anyone down in his life. Never.'

'I'm sure he wouldn't do it deliberately,' said Beulith. 'But he's never designed a set before. And regardless of what my father says, it's not easy. Just ask Rink Firsheen.'

'What would you like me to do?' asked Hermux. He could see that she was genuinely concerned.

'I want you to answer me honestly,' she said. 'Are you sure that you can really do it? And please tell me the truth. I can't

112

stand liars.' She looked intently at Hermux, her bright black eyes bulging with concentration.

Hermux considered her question carefully. After a long moment he spoke.

'No,' he said quietly. 'To be honest, I'm not sure I can do it. I told you that already. And your father. He thinks I can. And I certainly hope I can. And I'll try my hardest. But you're right. I've never designed a set before. I may fail. And that's the truth.'

Beulith smiled at him.

'Well, that's a relief,' she said.

'Then I don't get the job?' asked Hermux. He felt some relief himself.

'No, you've got the job. And I'm still worried about it. But at least it's a relief to know I can trust you. Most people are too conceited to tell the truth.'

Nip smiled. He was smitten.

'Here is the new contract,' said Beulith. 'It includes the set design and the original alarm-clock system. I tried to talk Dad out of that too. I can't see the point of it. But he's acting even more stubborn than usual.'

'He did seem very keen on the idea,' offered Hermux.

'I've used one of Hermux's alarm clocks for years,' Nip put in eagerly. 'Never had a problem with it. I'd be happy to bring it by the theatre if you'd like to see it.'

'That won't be necessary,' said Beulith. 'I'm sure Hermux does very good work. But it was sweet of you to offer.'

'At your service,' said Nip. He bowed.

'Well, then!' Beulith's nose blushed bright pink. 'Hermux, we'll expect you at the theatre Monday morning at nine. Dad says you plan to be there pretty much around the clock.'

'Did he?' said Hermux.

113

'Actually, it's in the contract, but don't worry. You won't be in the way. I'm setting you up with your own workspace in the basement.'

Beulith moved to leave. At the door she stopped.

'I hope I haven't discouraged you,' she said. 'I'm the worrier in the family. But Dad is probably right about you. He's almost always right about talent. You'll come through with the set.'

'And if you have any problems, don't hesitate to call me!' said Nip. He waved.

'Goodbye, Nip!' she said. She waved back.

'Well! Well! Well!' declared Nip as soon as she had gone. 'Hermux Tantamoq! Watchmaker! Detective! Ladies' mouse! *And* set designer! I've been wasting my time. I should have come back here years ago and studied with the master!'

Hermux wasn't listening to Nip's joke. He had just had a very unpleasant realization. In the weeks to come, he would be working long and late hours. And he hadn't said a word about it yet to Terfle.

Chapter 30
PEACE OFFERING

Terfle liked a regular schedule. And Hermux was usually a model of punctuality. It was one of the reasons they got along so well. Terfle was not going to like Hermux's working at the theatre one bit.

'Maybe I should buy her some flowers,' thought Hermux as he walked home along crowded Ferbosh Avenue. 'I bet she'd like that. A rosebud with real aphids would be perfect.' Hermux changed direction and headed downtown to Mrs Thankton's Florist Shop. It was a fine evening for a walk. It had rained that afternoon but cleared again. The clouds had moved north towards Twyrp, where Linka and Brinx were working.

'Brinx is going to film that fan club convention,' Hermux remembered. 'And the cemetery too.' He pictured the cemetery at night. It would be lonely there. Just the two of them. Rows of moonlit tombstones. Dark clouds scooting across the sky. And the ghost of Nurella Pinch wandering in the dark. Brinx breaks down and cries. Linka tries to comfort him. Brinx lays his head on her shoulder. And then –

'Keep your dirty paws off her!' growled Hermux through gritted teeth.

'Mind your own business!' replied a muscle-bound gerbil.

He and his girlfriend were waiting arm in arm for the light to change. 'Or I'll give you a black eye!'

'I'm sorry!' said Hermux. 'I must have been talking to myself.'

The girlfriend whispered something in the gerbil's ear. They both giggled. Next to them stood a jet black gerbil. He looked at Hermux and giggled too.

Hermux left them. He turned the corner and stopped.

'I'd better snap out of it,' he said. He shook his head and looked around. He was standing in front of Puppit's Pet Shop.

Right there in the front window he saw something truly marvellous.

It was a small cage beautifully made of brass wire. It had a carrying handle and a shoulder strap. And it came with two covers. One for summer and one for winter. The winter cover was persimmon velvet quilted in a diamond pattern. It zipped tight all around and had a tiny working porthole for looking in or out and for ventilation. The summer cover was a linen canvas the colour of fresh corn with apple green stripes. Each side could be rolled up and tied, and it had an awning with poles to shade the door.

Port-a-Pet Palace

FOR THE BUG ON THE GO!
ALL WEATHER! ALL SEASONS! STURDY CONSTRUCTION!

Open-plan design • Easy to clean • Easy to carry
Easy to store • Spill-proof water & food bowls • Heated perch*
Emergency bell • Area rug included • Optional hammock

*(requires two AAA batteries)

Hermux read the description with mounting excitement.

'It's perfect!' said Hermux.

And it was. He bought it and headed straight home.

'Terfle! Wake up and close your eyes!' he called as soon as he was inside the door. 'I've got a wonderful surprise for you!'

Terfle had not been sleeping. She was hungry and irritable. Hermux was late.

'Keep your eyes closed.' Hermux carried the Port-a-Pet Palace to his desk and set it down. It looked quite smart.

Hermux opened Terfle's cage.

'OK,' he said. He offered her his hand. 'But don't look. Please!'

He took her to his desk and lowered her gently.

'For you!' he said.

Terfle opened her eyes. She wasn't sure what to make of it.

'It's called the Port-a-Pet Palace,' Hermux explained, removing the velvet cover to reveal the interior. He opened the door. 'It's the de luxe model. Go on in! Take a look around. It has a heated perch and a bell for emergencies.'

Terfle sauntered forward.

'I'm going to be working at the Varmint Theatre for the next few weeks. I'll have to work late most nights. I got this so you could come to work with me. That way, you won't get so lonely.'

Terfle forgot about being hungry and irritable. She turned in the doorway. She looked up at Hermux and tapped her chest with a front leg. Right over her heart.

Hermux was very touched.

'I love you too!' he said. It felt good to say it. Plus, it was good practice. Even if it choked him up.

Chapter 31
MORNING COMMUTE

Stepping inside from the brilliant morning, it took a moment for Tucka Mertslin's eyes to adjust. Day or night, the dim light in the Greasy Griddle never changed. Neither did the air. They were both tired. Like the waitresses who had stood all night on their feet and still had an hour to go before their shifts ended. Like the customers who nursed their bottomless cups of weak coffee and pretended that they had jobs to go to and someone waiting for them at home.

'Hey, Tucka baby!' a voice called from a booth in the rear. A drab mouse in a tacky suit waved at her. 'I'm back here,' he said as though he expected her.

Tucka approached the booth with caution and apprehension. She wasn't accustomed to having unattractive people even speak to her, much less call her 'baby'. The mouse stopped buttering his toast and watched her with great interest.

'Glad to see me?' he asked.

'Who are you?' Tucka demanded. 'And where's Corpius? He was supposed to meet me here.'

'And Mr Crounce would never let you down,' the mouse said gallantly. He smiled his perfect smile and winked. It *was* Corpius Crounce.

'Oh! My! Gosh!' said Tucka. The floor seemed to buckle beneath her feet. She fell into the booth and burst into uncontrollable giggles. 'Look at you! You look awful!'

Crounce leaned across the table. 'Give me a kiss!' he said. 'A big sloppy one!'

'Stop it!' said Tucka. 'Or I'll scream!'

'Nobody around here will pay any attention,' he said. 'That's why I picked this place. A little privacy won't hurt us. Have you eaten?'

'No,' said Tucka. 'And I'm starved. What's good?'

'Try the hash browns. They're extra greasy.'

'Really?' she asked. She felt a tremor of guilty excitement as Crounce signalled the waitress. She couldn't take her eyes off him. Gone were his distinguished streaks and his natty goatee. Gone was the high-styled international playboy. In his place sat an indescribably ordinary mouse in a really bad suit.

Hot tears welled up in Tucka's eyes. Crounce was making an enormous sacrifice. And he was making it for her!

'I start work this morning at the Varmint Theatre,' he told her. 'Do I look like I fit in? The pay is lousy. But the benefits are excellent. Including the opportunity to snoop around!' He winked at her. 'Who knows? With a little luck I might end up owning the whole theatre.'

'You dear mouse! How can I ever repay you?'

'You're rich, aren't you?'

'Of course I am.'

'Then we'll think of something!'

Tucka mopped up the last of the ketchup with a forkful of hash browns.

'Corpius?' she said.

'Yes.'

119

'I have a little confession to make.'

'What is it, dear? Tell me everything.'

'I'm not a patient woman.'

'No?'

'No. I can get very cranky if I have to wait too long. I want the theatre soon.'

'How soon?'

'Next week.'

'I see.'

'I hoped you would.'

'Well? Then it looks like I'd better get to work.'

Tucka insisted on driving Crounce to the theatre. She wanted to drive him to the theatre door, but Crounce convinced her that it was unwise and made her stop the car on the side street to let him out.

'It's my man's first day at work,' she said. 'And to think that he's going to break the law for me! Now, that's what I call a crime of passion!'

Crounce pulled Tucka close to him and squeezed her tight. She puckered her lips. He puckered his. She was about to close her eyes when something on the street caught her attention. Abruptly she shoved Crounce away and lowered the dark glass window an inch.

'I don't like the looks of that at all,' she said, pointing down the street at the stage door entrance of the theatre.

Crounce joined her at the window.

'What's wrong?' he enquired.

'It's Hermux Tantamoq, the watchmaker who thinks he's a detective. He's going into the theatre. And what's he carrying?'

'It looks like a little travelling case.'

'Yellow and green stripes?' Tucka's eyes narrowed in suspicion. 'Something's wrong here. I can feel it. Tantamoq always means trouble.'

'Don't worry, I can take care of him,' Crounce assured her. 'Accidents are always happening backstage.'

Chapter 32
THE SET SHOP BOYS

Hermux nodded to the old gopher who sat beside the stage door.

'Good morning!' he said. 'Ms Varmint told me to meet her here at 9:00. I'm Hermux Tantamoq, the watchmaker. I'm going to be working here. And this is Terfle.' He held up Terfle's travelling cage. 'She's a ladybird.'

Beulith arrived shortly after and led Hermux through a maze of corridors and down a twisting flight of stairs to the basement.

Hermux followed her into a large cluttered room that smelled of sawdust and glue and turpentine. From the ceiling hung chandeliers, streetlamps, painted moons and massive clown heads with big staring eyes. Stacked along the walls were statues and jewelled thrones and ancient columns. There were racks of saws and hammers and drills. Piles of lumber. Cans of paint. And bins full of nuts and bolts and nails. At a bench in the back sat three chipmunks. They leapt to their feet when they saw Beulith.

'Good morning, Ms Varmint! We were just about to start!' said the first.

'That's right! Just getting going!' confirmed the second.

'Absolutely! Ready to work!' added the third.

122

Beulith introduced them. 'Hermux, this is Sputter, Gnawton and Chizzel. They're our carpenters and stagehands. And despite their appearance, they are very hard workers.'

'And we can build anything!' bragged Sputter.

'Any size!' bragged Gnawton.

'Any shape!' bragged Chizzel.

'Any material!' they bragged in chorus.

'Just draw us a picture!'

'Or a plan!'

'Or build us a model!'

'And we take it from there,' they sang in unison. 'We cut it out! We carve it! We glue it! We wire it! We nail it!'

'Thank you, gentlemen,' said Beulith. 'And this is Hermux Tantamoq. He's a watchmaker, and Dad has hired him to install alarm clocks in all the shops and dressing rooms.'

'Why?' asked Sputter. He folded his arms over his chest, flicked his tail up to its full extension and stuck his chin out stubbornly. 'We're never late!'

'Never!' repeated Gnawton.

'Ever!' added Chizzel.

'Of course you're not,' Beulith conceded diplomatically. 'It's more for the performers.'

'Oh,' they said.

'And Hermux is also going to be designing the set for the *Silver Jubilee*.'

'That's better!' said Sputter.

'Much!' said Gnawton. 'If there's anything you need, just tell us!'

'Anything at all!' they sang together.

'Thank you,' said Hermux. 'I will. I have a lot to learn about set design.'

Sputter, Gnawton and Chizzel exchanged puzzled looks.

Beulith grabbed Hermux by the elbow and said, 'Let me show you where you'll be working, Hermux. There's a space just across the hall.' She led him quickly away.

Hermux's workspace was a small, empty storeroom next to the costume shop. Hermux set down the Port-a-Pet.

'Are those all the tools you brought?' asked Beulith.

'Oh, these aren't tools.' Hermux removed the Port-a-Pet's summer cover. 'Nip is bringing the tools over later. This is Terfle. She's my pet ladybird. She gets lonely at home, so I brought her with me.'

'Welcome to the Varmint!' Beulith said to Terfle.

Terfle looked up at her uncertainly.

'She may be a little shy at first,' said Hermux. 'It's her first time in a theatre.'

'She's very pretty.'

'Thank you,' said Hermux. 'She's also very smart. She loves maps.'

'I don't have any maps,' said Beulith. 'But I did bring you a floor plan of the theatre. Dad wanted me to give it to you. She might like that.'

'She might very well,' said Hermux.

'May I come in?' asked a friendly voice. An older mouse stood in the open doorway. She wore an apron covered with pockets and stuck full of pins. A pair of scissors hung from a ribbon around her neck. She had a pleasant face and bright, inquisitive eyes.

'Glissin!' Beulith greeted the visitor affectionately. 'Of course! Come in and meet Hermux Tantamoq. He's going to be your neighbour for a while. He's installing alarm clocks for us. And then he's going to be designing the set for the *Spectacular.*

Hermux, this is Glissin. She's our costume mistress. And my dearest friend!'

'I'm very pleased to meet you,' said Glissin. 'Clocks *and* sets. That's an unusual combination.'

'Hermux is a very unusual mouse,' said Beulith somewhat awkwardly. 'He's just getting started in set design.'

'Oh, is he?' asked Glissin. 'And who's this?' She knelt over the Port-a-Pet.

'That's Terfle,' said Beulith. 'Hermux's pet.'

'What a beautiful bug!' said Glissin. 'I hope she and I can be friends!'

Terfle bowed deeply and waved an antenna.

'She likes you already,' said Hermux.

'And I like her,' said Glissin, stroking the cage lightly. 'Once you're settled in, why don't you come over to my studio? I'm just next door. And bring Terfle with you. I'll make us some tea.'

'Why, thank you!' said Hermux. 'I never say no to a hot beverage.'

'And when you get a chance, Dad wants to see you in his office,' Beulith told Hermux. 'To go over some details.'

Nip delivered Hermux's tools on schedule and then hurried back to the shop, disappointed that he didn't get to see Beulith. Hermux and Terfle visited Glissin for tea. And then Terfle stayed behind at Glissin's invitation while Hermux kept his appointment with Varmint.

Varmint was impatient. 'What have you found out?'

'Nothing yet. I'm just getting settled.'

'Well, stop wasting time! While you were getting settled, I got this.' He waved another note under Hermux's nose. 'Someone slipped it under my door.'

Hermux read it. It was another warning. It said that

125

Varmint's time at the theatre was running out fast.

'It's somebody inside,' said Varmint. 'I told you. You've got to be careful what you say. Don't trust anyone here! Anyone!'

That worried Hermux. He had just left Terfle with Glissin, who, after all, was practically a stranger, despite the fact that she made a very good cup of tea. 'Does that include Glissin?' he asked.

'Not Glissin! The others! Glissin is practically family. She was a friend of my wife's. She's been almost a mother to Beulith since –' His voice died away.

'And what about Oaf?' asked Hermux.

'Don't be stupid!' said Varmint. 'Oaf's been with me forever. Besides, he has no imagination. It's the performers you've got to watch. They're the sneaky ones!' He punched his intercom.

'Yes, Dad?' Beulith's voice crackled through the speaker.

'Would you get the cast together in the green room this afternoon and introduce them to Hermux? It's time he finds out who he's dealing with.'

Varmint sat back, looking very pleased with himself.

'You can give me a full report tomorrow.'

'On what?' Hermux asked.

'On what you find out in the meantime. And I need to see drawings for the set. We're all counting on you, Tantamoq. Time's running out.'

Chapter 33
ALARMING INFORMATION

The green room was the performers' lounge. It was where actors snacked and napped; where chorus squirrels gossiped while they darned their tights; and where Furry and Findler had some of their loudest arguments. Beulith gathered the whole cast there to meet Hermux.

She concluded her introduction, 'Naturally the installation may entail some disruption and inconvenience, but we hope that you will all give Mr Tantamoq your full cooperation. Are there any questions?'

'Yes,' said a plumpish field mouse with heavy eyebrows and extremely intense eyes. 'May I ask what the point of this alarm-clock system is? I have never been late for anything in my whole life.'

'The point is, Tector . . .' Beulith began. 'The point is . . . I think it might be better if Hermux explained it himself.'

Hermux looked out at the roomful of expectant faces. He recognized a few of them. He remembered that Tector Serfinch was a hypnotist. And a mind-reader. He would have to be careful around him. He thought he recognized the flirty chorus squirrel. He might have to be careful around her too. And in the last row of chairs sat the ventriloquist. Next to him was a homely sort of mouse in a shiny green suit.

'Nice suit!' thought Hermux. The ventriloquist leaned over to the mouse and whispered something in his ear. The mouse nodded in agreement.

'Hermux?' reminded Beulith. 'Could you say a few words about the alarm clocks?'

'Oh! Yes!' said Hermux. He cleared his throat. 'The alarm clock is one of the great inventions of modern clockmaking. With a good alarm clock at our side, it is possible to face the most demanding schedule with absolute confidence, knowing that we will always be on time –'

Hermux was very enthusiastic when it came to alarm clocks. He thought he made a very persuasive case for them.

But apparently not everyone agreed.

When he returned to his workspace, Hermux found a note taped to his door.

Mind your own business!
Or your *little* bug friend bites
the big one!

A Friend

Chapter 34
FROM THE TERRACE

The costume shop was the social centre of the Varmint, and by midafternoon Terfle thought that she must have met everyone who worked at the theatre. Performers came and went for fittings and repairs. Varmint dropped by to see sketches. And Beulith popped in any time she was in the vicinity. At lunch a group of regulars from the cast and crew joined Glissin for sandwiches and a friendly game of cards. Terfle learned her first magic trick from a magician. She got an introductory lesson from the hypnotist. And she met the ventriloquist and his new apprentice. It was an exciting day.

Glissin proved to be an excellent companion. She showed Terfle all around her workshop. The fabric room, the cutting tables, the sewing machines and the dummies in a variety of body types. Terfle's favourite part of all was the cabinet of drawers filled with buttons of every shape and sequins in every colour of the rainbow.

Glissin loved her job, and she did it very well. When she wasn't sewing costumes, she used to amuse herself by making dolls' clothes and sock puppets and stuffed insects. Then a year ago, Sputter, Gnawton and Chizzel had surprised her by building her a doll's house. It was really more a doll mansion than a house. It was two storeys tall with chimneys and an imitation flagstone terrace.

Glissin christened it the Villa de Varmint. She was very proud of it, and now she devoted most of her spare time to making improvements. She made curtains, rugs and wallpaper for each of the rooms. She made tables, couches and chairs. She painted miniature paintings to hang on the walls.

Glissin gave Terfle a complete tour of the villa. At the end of the tour she told Terfle that, while she was at the theatre, she should think of the Villa de Varmint as her home away from home. Terfle accepted the invitation immediately. She headed straight up the stairs to the master bedroom. She closed the curtains and crawled into the four-poster queen-sized bed. She had had enough excitement for one day. It was time for a nap.

Hermux's voice woke her. At first she didn't know where she was. She didn't recall having satin sheets at home. Then she remembered. She was at the theatre. She was Glissin's guest at the Villa de Varmint.

'Terfle!' shouted Hermux. 'Terfle! Where are you? Are you all right?'

From the tone of his voice Terfle knew something was wrong. She got up from the bed, smoothed the covers back in place and made her way down the curving staircase to the main floor. She passed through the formal dining room, its table set with china and crystal for twelve and she stepped out on to the terrace. It was still under construction. The flagstones were drawn in place but not painted. The hedge, made of kitchen sponges, still needed to be dyed and trimmed. A string of paper lanterns lay in a heap, waiting to be hung. Terfle scuttled to the edge of the terrace and waved.

'What's the matter?' asked Glissin, rushing from the fabric room with a bolt of muslin under her arm.

'Where's Terfle?' asked Hermux. 'What's happened to her?'

'Why, I think she's asleep,' said Glissin. She led Hermux to the table that held the villa. 'There she is! On the terrace.'

'Terfle! Thank goodness!' Hermux knelt down and tapped her gently. Terfle opened her elytra, stretched her wings briefly and yawned. She hadn't quite finished her nap.

'What on earth did you think had happened?' asked Glissin. 'It's been a very quiet day down here.'

Hermux didn't answer immediately. Overhead the stage floor rumbled and creaked as the chorus squirrels twirled through a rehearsal. Varmint and Beulith evidently trusted Glissin. And she certainly seemed kindly and helpful. But Hermux had recently learned that appearances can be deceptive. And now he had entered a new and unfamiliar world. A world of illusions within illusions. He knew he would need allies to survive.

He gave Glissin the note.

'I found this on my door.'

Chapter 35
WHAT'S IN A NAME?

Two burly woodchucks struggled to manoeuvre a big crate into the elevator at Hermux's apartment building.

'What floor?' asked Hermux, trying to get out of their way.

'Four,' said one.

'Same as me,' said Hermux. He pushed the button. 'What do you have there? It's kind of late for deliveries, isn't it?'

'Don't know,' said one.

'Don't care,' said the other.

When the elevator opened on four, it was met by Rink Firsheen.

'Be careful with that!' Rink ordered the deliverymen. 'It's fragile!'

'Where's it go?' asked one.

Rink looked at Tucka for an answer. She was standing in the open door of her apartment.

'Set it up in the dining room,' she said. 'We'll have more room to work there. I can't wait to see it!' Tucka clapped her hands with glee. However, her high spirits vanished immediately when she saw Hermux emerge from the elevator behind the crate.

'What did you get?' he asked in a nice, neighbourly way.

'None of your business!' she said. She ushered the deliverymen inside.

Rink joined her in the doorway. 'Tantamoq!' he chortled. 'Be sure to call me if you have any questions about set design!'

Rink and Tucka burst into laughter, and Tucka slammed the door.

'Let's get to work!' she said.

The crate was placed in the centre of Tucka's enormous dining-room table.

'If you scratched that table, you're buying it!' Tucka warned the woodchucks.

'Ssssh!' said Rink. Carefully he removed the top of the crate. And then the sides, one by one. 'Voilà!'

Tucka stared in amazement.

'What do you think?' asked Rink. 'I did it all in one day!'

'Gee!' said one of the woodchucks. 'What is it?'

'Get out! Both of you!' Tucka told them. 'You're done here.' She escorted them to the door, pushed them out into the hall and locked the door behind them. Then she rushed back to the dining room.

'Rink! You're a genius!' she twittered. 'An absolute genius!'

'I know,' he said, beaming.

There on Tucka's dining-room table stood a full-colour, scale model of the Varmint Variety Theatre. But there was more. To give it a sense of context, Rink had built the entire block of buildings that surrounded the theatre. It was extremely impressive.

'Let me get my supplies, and we can get started.' Rink was back in a moment with a suitcase. He opened it and removed rolls of masking tape, utility knives and extra blades, drawing

133

pins, bottles of glue, sheets of cardboard, rulers, markers, paints, brushes and a hairdryer. 'That should be everything. What do you want to do first?'

Tucka gazed rapturously at the theatre.

'I hardly know where to begin.'

'You'll think of something,' Rink said.

'Well, I've never cared much for the name,' she said, pointing at the theatre's marquee. 'Could we do something about that?'

'How about this?' Rink sprang forward, grasping the theatre's marquee in both paws. He ripped it loose and threw it on the floor. He prised open a can of white paint, loaded up a brush and in one fat stroke VARMINT, VARIETY AND THEATRE vanished from sight. He plugged in the hairdryer and blew the paint dry. Then, with a number 10 round sable brush and a tube of paint labelled ALIZARIN CRIMSON, he painstakingly lettered:

TUCKA MERTSLIN'S MAJESTIC THEATRE

'One of the few nice things you can say about sables,' Rink remarked when he had finished. 'They do make the best brushes. So what do you think? Better?'

'I'm beginning to see the potential,' said Tucka reverently. 'Mertslin's Majestic . . . it does have a nice sound to it. But –'

'But what?' asked Rink.

'I don't know,' sighed Tucka. 'It just needs something.'

'How about this?' Rink added two lines of text.

TUCKA MERTSLIN'S MAJESTIC THEATRE
STARRING
TUCKA MERTSLIN

Tucka hummed. 'That's better! Now I'm liking it. I'm liking it a lot. But something is still missing.'

'I think I know what you mean,' said Rink. He looked around the room for inspiration. Over the fireplace hung an enormous portrait of Tucka. 'I've got it!' he shouted. 'Close your eyes!' He grabbed the brush and began painting again. When he finished, he set the marquee back on the front of the theatre and snapped it in place. 'OK. You can look now.'

TUCKA MERTSLIN'S MAJESTIC THEATRE
STARRING
TUCKA MERTSLIN
IN ME!

'Yes!' said Tucka. 'Yes!' She stepped back and admired their work. Then she frowned. 'What's that awful thing?' she asked. She pointed at the model.

'It's a hardware store.'

'I hate it!'

Rink opened a can of white spray paint. In moments the hardware store sign was gone.

'I hate that too!' said Tucka. She pointed at the drugstore next door.

Rink sprayed, and it vanished.

'And that!'

Soon the entire block except for the theatre was whited out.

'Now what?' asked Rink.

'Sssssh! I'm thinking,' she said. 'Give me that brush!' Tucka began to paint. Above the window of what had been the dry cleaner, a new sign appeared.

I Dream of Tucka
Fashions for the woman who wants everything she has!

'Think retail!' she told Rink.

'I am,' he said. 'How about this?' He added a new logo above the drugstore.

Tucka at Home
Modern Designs for the Upwardly Mobile

'I could go on and on!' said Tucka.

'Why don't we?'

In twenty minutes the entire block was covered with Tucka's name.

'Is there anything we've forgotten?' she asked.

'Let's see,' said Rink. 'Clothes, shoes, hats, jewellery, flowers, gifts, furniture, gardening, kitchen, bath, bedroom, toys and art. What about insurance?'

'Insurance bores me!'

'Then I think we're done.'

They were interrupted by the ringing of the telephone.

It was Crounce. Tucka asked him to hold the line.

'It's an admirer,' she explained to Rink, batting her eyes seductively. She took the phone into her bedroom and closed the door. 'My darling,' she said. 'What's up?'

'Good news, my luscious little apricot!'

'What?' Tucka moaned in anticipation.

'While he was rehearsing this afternoon, I paid a visit to Varmint's office. I found something I think will interest you. Hidden in the safe.'

'Tell me!' she begged.

'I think it would be better to show you. How about lunch tomorrow? The Swank and Swill?'

'I wouldn't miss it for the world.'

'I didn't think so,' Crounce crooned. 'Until tomorrow then. Sweet dreams!'

'Sweet dreams to you too! My dearest!'

'Wait!' said Crounce. 'I almost forgot! You don't need to worry about your irritating little watchmaker friend. I found out what he's doing at the theatre. He's installing alarm clocks for Varmint. But just for good measure I gave him a little scare. I don't think he'll be giving us any trouble any time soon.'

Chapter 36
LA VIDA LOCA

Hermux was adamant.

'Something bad is going on there. It's too dangerous for you. I want you home where I know you're safe.'

But Terfle could be adamant too. She had had a wonderful day at the theatre, and she wanted more. Besides, Glissin wanted her to help with the costumes and Tector the hypnotist had promised her another lesson. Terfle gave Hermux her steeliest look and shook her head.

'Try to understand!' Hermux asked. 'It's for your own good.'

Terfle pushed her food bowl away without touching a bite.

'Please!' begged Hermux.

Terfle responded by turning her back on him.

Finally Hermux relented. 'But if you come,' he insisted, 'you have to swear that you'll stay close to me or Glissin. And if you see anything suspicious, you let me know immediately.'

Terfle nodded her agreement. Then she hurried back to her dinner. She was relieved that she wasn't going to have to go hungry. It had been a long day. As soon as she finished eating, she got ready for bed.

Bed sounded like a good idea to Hermux too. But once

snuggled in, he couldn't help thinking back over the events of the tumultuous day. He opened his journal and wrote.

> *Thank you for the handy Port-a-Pet Palace with the de luxe options package. It has opened up an exciting new world for Terfle. Please don't make me regret buying it. Thank you for set shops and stagehands and particularly for trustworthy costume mistresses.*
>
> *P.S. I would be very grateful for any help or inspiration you might have concerning set design.*

Hermux had closed his journal and was capping his pen when the phone rang.

'Who could be calling at this hour?' He hoped it wasn't a threatening call.

'Hermux?' Her voice sounded far away.

'Linka!' He nearly shouted. 'Are you home?'

'No. We're in Woodland. We came here straight from Twyrp. We're staying at the Woodland Hills Hotel! Where the stars stay! I've got my own private bungalow right by the pool.'

Hermux tried to visualize Linka in a bungalow, surrounded by movie stars. But all the stars looked like Brinx Lotelle. And they were leering at Linka.

'That sounds exciting,' he said. 'How is it working with Brinx?'

'It's fascinating. He knows everybody in Woodland,' she enthused. 'We filmed all day at Graffini Studios. I even met the president of the studio. We interviewed him in Nurella Pinch's old dressing room. They've kept it exactly as she left it. Then we went to the back lot. They've still got some of the original sets from her films. I even climbed up into the tree house from *Nozelle:*

She-Mouse of the Jungle. Brinx photographed me. Then he got the wildest idea. You won't believe it.'

'What?' asked Hermux unhappily. He braced himself for the worst.

'He wants me to take a screen test.'

Hermux thought about it. Maybe it was the worst.

'Isn't that thrilling?' Linka asked.

'I guess so,' Hermux conceded. 'Are you going to do it?'

'Of course I am! We're shooting it tomorrow. Brinx wants me to start with a love scene.'

'Of course he does!' Hermux muttered under his breath.

'And I'm so nervous! But Brinx says not to worry. He's shot hundreds of love scenes.'

'I'm sure he has!'

'And he's going to coach me through it himself! Isn't that fantastic?'

'You took the words right out of my mouth,' professed Hermux. 'It's utterly fantastic. It boggles the mind.'

'And how are things going at the theatre?' asked Linka. 'Are you making any progress?'

'It's hard to say,' Hermux began. 'So far, it's kind of confusing.'

There was pounding in the background.

'Hermux? I'm afraid I've got to go. Brinx is having a pool party for some people he wants me to meet.'

'Isn't it late to be swimming?' enquired Hermux. It was nearly ten o'clock.

'Don't be silly!' she scolded. 'This is Woodland! The pools here are heated and lighted. People swim whenever they want to.'

Chapter 37
A Kiss Is Just a Kiss

The first plane to Woodland left Pinchester at dawn. Hermux was on it. When it landed at Woodland International Airport, Hermux raced down the loading ramp and sprinted across the lobby. He found a taxi waiting at the kerb outside. He leapt inside.

'Graffini Studios, and step on it!' he told the driver.

The taxi sped away, weaving its way wildly through the rush-hour traffic.

A triumphal arch with massive wrought-iron gates formed the main entrance to the studio lot. The gates were closed. As they approached, a guard stepped out of the security booth and waved them to a stop.

'ID, please,' he told Hermux.

Hermux opened his wallet. He handed the guard a business card.

'A watchmaker, huh? We don't get many watchmakers.'

'Brinx Lotelle wants to see me right away,' Hermux lied. 'It's important!'

'He's filming on Soundstage A,' the guard said. 'I'll have to call him.'

'Fine!' Hermux lied again. 'He's expecting me.' As soon as the guard was gone, Hermux removed a hundred-dollar bill from his wallet. He tossed it into the driver's lap. 'I've got another one just like this if you get me inside the gate.'

The driver examined the bill. It was real.

'All right, mister!' he said. 'Fasten your seat belt!' He revved the engine. Then released the brake. The taxi crashed through the gate and raced forward.

'Straight ahead!' Hermux shouted. 'Soundstage A!'

The taxi screeched to a stop at the back of the lot. Hermux threw the driver another hundred-dollar bill and leapt out. The door to the soundstage was rolled open. Three chipmunks were struggling to maneuver an enormous crate inside. Hermux slipped past them and found himself inside a dark and cavernous space.

In the far corner Hermux could see bright lights.

'Places on the set!' someone announced.

'Tell them I'll be there in a minute,' a familiar voice commanded. It was Brinx Lotelle. Hermux was standing right outside his dressing room. The door with Brinx's name and a big gold star was closed.

'Yes, sir!' answered Hermux. 'I will.' He looked around for something to block the door with. A huge cabinet stood to one side. But Hermux couldn't move it. There was a latch on Brinx's door. 'If only I had some wire,' thought Hermux. 'I could lock him in.' But he couldn't find any wire. He checked the pockets of his trenchcoat and was astounded to find a padlock of all things. 'This will work!' he thought. He snapped it quickly in place, then hurried to the set.

Facing an enormous camera, Linka stood alone on a fake balcony that overlooked a panoramic painting of a night-time city. A wind machine teased the gauzy fabric of her evening gown. A single spotlight focused on her uplifted face. She waited expectantly, her enormous eyes calm and luminous.

'Are you ready, Ms Perflinger?' the cameraman asked.

'Ready,' she said.

'Mr Lotelle?' he asked.

'I'm ready too,' said Hermux. 'Roll camera!' He strode on to the balcony and seized Linka in his arms. Her eyes opened wide. 'Surprised to see me?' he asked. Then he leaned her ever so gently back against the balcony rail and pressed his lips to hers.

'Oh, Hermux!' she exclaimed. 'You're here!'

'And I'm not leaving! I love you, Linka! I love you!'

'Cut!' someone yelled. A bell clanged furiously. 'Cut! That's not in the script!'

But Hermux didn't stop.

'I love you!' he swore faithfully. 'I love you!'

The bell didn't stop ringing either.

Not until Hermux reached out a sleepy paw and switched off his alarm clock.

Chapter 38
POLLY WANTS A CRACKER

The floor plan of the theatre was spread out on Hermux's worktable at the theatre. Hermux leaned forward, propped on his elbows, and watched Terfle's progress. She crawled across the stage and then turned and skirted the side, pausing momentarily at each of the dressing-room doors. She passed the chorus squirrels' door, the hypnotist's, the magician's and the ventriloquist's. Then she seemed to have second thoughts. She retraced her steps to the dressing room labelled GILDEN BINTER – VENTRILOQUIST. Slowly, carefully, she stepped over the threshold.

'I think you're right,' observed Hermux. 'I've got a funny feeling about him too. That's where I'll start. But first I'll get you settled with Glissin. She wants you to help her sewing sequins.'

Terfle raised a front leg and pointed at Hermux. She looked quickly over both her shoulders, then pointed again at Hermux.

'Don't worry!' he assured her. 'I'll be careful too.'

Hermux left Terfle with Glissin. Then he gathered his toolbox and a roll of alarm-clock wire and went upstairs. Onstage Sputter, Gnawton and Chizzel were noisily adjusting lights. But offstage the area of the dressing rooms was deserted. Hermux tapped on Gilden's door. There was no response. The

144

door was locked. So Hermux used the passkey that Varmint had given him. He unlocked the door and slipped inside.

The room was pitch-black and silent as a tomb. Hermux could hear his heart pounding in his ears. He sniffed suspiciously. A sour stench hung heavy in the air.

'Something rotten is going on here!' thought Hermux. He felt a sudden premonition. The unsettling sense that the room wasn't empty. Someone else was there. He ran his hand lightly across the wall, searching for the light switch.

A nasty hiss broke the silence. 'Try the other side, you little creep!' It was Gilden Binter's voice.

Hermux found the switch and flicked it on.

He turned sharply and found himself face-to-face with the parrot.

The parrot screeched, 'Who did you expect? Nurella Pinch?' Gilden Binter was nowhere in sight.

Hermux couldn't help himself, he dropped his toolbox on his foot. 'Aaaaaagh!' he screamed, half in fear, half in pain.

The parrot rocked from side to side on his perch and examined Hermux with a cold eye. 'The nervous type, huh? Maybe you should consider a new line of work. A burglar needs to be quiet.'

'I was quiet!' Hermux protested. 'Besides, I am not a burglar. I have a key.' He held up the passkey. 'What are you doing in here, anyway?'

'I work here,' said the parrot. 'Remember?'

The parrot was right.

'But that doesn't explain why you can talk,' said Hermux. He thought he had the upper hand there. 'You're supposed to be a dummy. The programme says *ventriloquist*!'

'Do you see my lips moving?' the parrot asked. He was clearly amused by the situation.

'You don't have lips!' said Hermux.

'That's my point!' boomed the parrot in a perfect imitation of Fluster Varmint. 'Take my word for it, son. Parrots make the best ventriloquists!'

Hermux felt a little confused.

'You have anything to eat?' the parrot asked. 'I'm sick of this garbage!' Beneath his perch lay a heap of banana peels, wilted vegetables and mouldy fruit.

'So, if you're providing the voices, what does Binter do?'

'Collects the pay cheque!' squawked the parrot.

'But you're doing all the work!'

'Bingo!' said the parrot. 'The mouse shows signs of intelligent life.'

'Then what's in it for you?'

'A life of luxury!' the parrot said bitterly. 'What are you snooping around for, anyway?'

'I'm not snooping. I'm installing alarm clocks.'

'I doubt it! You're looking for something.'

Hermux pointed to his toolbox as proof.

'Any food in that? Crackers? Nuts? Cheese? You look like you get your share.'

'No,' answered Hermux. 'Just tools.' He sucked in his stomach.

'You know, you should be nice to me.' The parrot took on a chummy tone. 'I could help you out. There's some pretty funny stuff going on around here. And I hear it all.'

'Then you know who's sending the threatening notes?' The words came tumbling out of Hermux's mouth faster than he could stop them.

'So it's threatening notes, is it?' the parrot crowed. It flapped its wings and stretched a leg. 'How corny can they get?'

146

'What do you know about it?'

'What'll you pay?'

Hermux thought fast.

'A bag of dry-roasted, salted peanuts.'

'Almonds, and you got a deal!' the parrot bargained.

'OK, almonds,' Hermux conceded. 'Now, tell me what you know!'

The sound of a key in the lock silenced the parrot. Its eyes shut instantly. Its body froze in place. As the door to the dressing room swung open, Hermux dived for his toolbox. He grabbed the tape measure and threw himself out full length on the floor.

'Who left the light on?' It was the ventriloquist.

'That's eight feet and six inches exactly,' Hermux announced loudly. 'From the door to the counter.' He looked up in pretended surprise. Gilden Binter and his apprentice glowered down at him.

'Can you hand me that roll of wire?' Hermux asked.

'What are you doing here?' the apprentice demanded. His broad shoulders in the shiny green suit looked quite menacing from Hermux's angle.

'Alarm clocks,' answered Hermux, attempting a smile. 'Just getting some measurements before I start installing. I can come back later if you want.'

'Not so fast,' said Binter. 'How'd you get in here?'

'The door was open,' said Hermux.

'Not!' said Binter. 'It was locked. I never leave it unlocked! Never! Never! Never!' His voice got shrill, then shriller.

'Calm down,' the apprentice advised Binter. 'There's no reason to act paranoid. Mr Tantamoq has work to do.' His observant eyes bored into Hermux. 'Maybe *I* left it open.'

Binter turned on him. 'Well, don't do it again!' he snarled.

'A dummy like Termind is impossible to replace.'

'I'll be more careful in the future,' the apprentice apologized. He smoothed the iridescent feathers on Termind's head. 'We'll all be more careful. It would be horrible if something happened to Termind. Wouldn't it, Mr Tantamoq?'

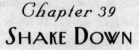

Chapter 39
SHAKE DOWN

When Hermux got back to his workroom, Oaf was waiting for him.

'There's going to be a production meeting for the *Silver Jubilee* this afternoon,' he said. 'Varmint wants you to bring the drawings for the set.'

'The set?' asked Hermux. 'Oh, sure. No problem.' He had forgotten all about it. 'What time?'

'About three.'

That gave Hermux less than four hours to design his first stage set. When Oaf left, Hermux opened his sketchbook to page one. It was blank like all the others. He sharpened a pencil. And sat. A half-hour later, the page was still empty.

It wasn't because Hermux didn't have an imagination. He was certainly imagining things as he stared at his pencil and sketchbook. He was imagining Brinx and Linka alone in her aeroplane. He was imagining someone plotting to destroy Fluster Varmint. And a parrot with a secret to tell. But he wasn't imagining a stage full of dancing squirrels.

He looked around the bare basement room.

'Maybe what I need is inspiration.' Hermux wondered what

Mirrin would do in a similar situation. He pictured her in her studio with her vase of roses. 'She would look before she painted.' It made perfect sense. If he was going to design something for the stage, maybe he should start by looking at the stage.

The auditorium was deserted. Hermux found himself a seat in the first row in the centre of the balcony. He felt strangely peaceful sitting there by himself in the darkness. A velvety, luxurious silence filled the air. Hermux looked down on the empty stage and waited for inspiration.

Minutes passed. Nothing happened.

Hermux closed his eyes and tried to empty his mind of all thoughts. After a time it seemed that in the far distance of his imagination a shadowy shape began to take form.

Hermux tried to stay calm.

'I'm actually having an inspiration!' he thought.

The shape grew larger. It filled the darkness with an immense and overwhelming presence. It radiated pure power and energy. Then it revealed itself to Hermux. Clear as daylight. Solid as a house. Splendid. Magnificent.

A doughnut. Chocolate at first. Then coconut. Then celery. It was the sum of all doughnuts.

Hermux was amazed.

A deep, low growl interrupted his reverie. Startled, Hermux opened his eyes. His ears at full attention.

Another growl. It wasn't his imagination. It was his stomach.

Hermux was so disappointed that he vowed to himself to sit there in the theatre until he had a genuine inspiration. He would sit there forever if that's what it took.

And perhaps if he hadn't made that vow at that very moment,

he wouldn't have been listening quite so hard to the silence that followed. And he wouldn't have noticed what sounded like very stealthy footsteps climbing the balcony stairs behind him.

Hermux listened again. He wasn't imagining it. There were definitely footsteps. And they were definitely stealthy. They were more than stealthy; they were sneaky. Not the firm, careless footsteps of someone going about their regular job. They were careful and slightly irregular, as though someone were feeling their way in the dark. And making an effort to make as little noise as possible.

'Well,' thought Hermux, 'two can play this game.' He took great pride in his own stealthy walking. He slid from his seat and very carefully eased its bottom back into place without letting it squeak.

The stairs rose steeply to the top of the theatre. Halfway up, a passageway led back to the balcony lobby and lounges. Cupping his ears to hear better, Hermux made out a faint creak high above him. He ascended the steps as quickly as he dared. He didn't want to bump into the intruder accidentally. He wasn't even sure it was an intruder. Maybe sneaking around in the dark was something that theatre people normally did.

But if they did, Hermux was fairly certain that they didn't open doors in the creepy one-click-at-a-time way that he heard the door at the top of the stairs being opened.

A dim light momentarily outlined the open door. Hermux glimpsed a shadowy figure slipping through and pulling the door closed behind it. Hermux hurried to the door. He cautiously placed his paw on the knob and then, one careful click at a time, he turned it, eased the door open a crack, and slipped through.

He found himself in a narrow passageway that ran along the outside wall of the theatre. It ended in a short flight of iron stairs.

Warily Hermux mounted. The stairs joined a narrow bridge that vanished in the space between the roof of the building and the ceiling of the theatre. Hermux could feel the vibrations of someone moving along the bridge. The whole structure swayed slightly in the darkness. It was not a nice feeling. The only illumination, a single bare bulb hanging somewhere back above the stage, threw more shadow than light. It was difficult to see where the edges of the bridge ended and empty space began. Below that empty space, Hermux knew, was suspended the elaborately carved plaster ceiling of the auditorium. Below that there was nothing but more empty space, and plenty of it, until you reached the floor. Or hit it, if you fell. He didn't want to think about that now. He edged forward nimbly, feeling his way among the electric cables that snaked and coiled along the bridge.

About halfway across, Hermux heard a furtive rustle and someone breathing. It was creepily close.

'Excuse me!' he called out. 'Who's there?'

There was one more rustle, and then it stopped.

'Hello?' called Hermux. 'What are you doing up here?'

There was no answer. The bridge suddenly jerked violently from side to side. Hermux felt himself losing his balance and would have fallen right over the edge if his tail hadn't wedged so firmly in a bundle of cables. He righted himself and instinctively dropped to his hands and knees. It was a sensible move. And lucky too. Because without warning the bridge bounced straight up into the air and would have handily tossed him off if he had been standing. Instead, it flattened him and merely knocked the breath out of him. Hermux realized that the stealthy visitor was jumping up and down on the bridge to try to knock him off. He held on even more tightly. The jumping dislodged a coil of cable that fell with a sickening crash.

152

'Oww!' yelled Hermux, pretending to have fallen. 'Help! I can't move! I think I broke my legs.'

Hermux felt a rumble along the bridge. He struggled to his feet, bracing himself for the impending collision. His assailant walked right into him. The impact nearly pitched Hermux from the bridge.

'What the –'

Hermux grabbed blindly. His hands closed on a powerful arm. The arm shook free. Hermux scrabbled for another grip. His hands found fur. A mouse's head. Then a knee struck Hermux hard in the stomach. He doubled over and collapsed, panting, on the bridge.

'Broke your legs, huh?' his assailant taunted. 'Next time I'll break your neck!'

Hermux heard the door to the balcony bang open and closed. Then the theatre was silent again.

Chapter 40
ACCOUNTS PAYABLE

Crounce was late for lunch, and Tucka was miffed.

'I've been waiting for twenty minutes,' she said, pouting, when he finally arrived. 'I told you at the beginning that I'm not a patient woman.'

'I had to find somewhere to change clothes,' he explained. 'I wasn't quite dressed for the Swank and Swill.'

'You're still not,' Tucka whispered. She gestured towards her left ear.

Crounce patted his own ear. Surprised at what he found, he pretended to give his ear a good scratching. When he was done, he slipped something dark and furry into his pocket. 'Sorry,' he said. 'I was interrupted by that little snoop Tantamoq.'

'What did he want?' asked Tucka. 'Does he suspect something?'

'Of course not. What could he possibly suspect? I think he's just naturally nosy. I've never liked nosy mice.'

'Keep an eye on him, Corpius. I know him, and I don't trust him. He's never up to any good.'

'I intend to. But right now I'd rather keep an eye on you!' He licked his lips. Then his eyes widened in apparent shock.

'Don't move!' he ordered. 'Don't move a muscle! Just sit very, very still!'

Tucka went rigid with fear. 'It's not a wasp, is it? I'm terribly allergic.'

'No,' breathed Crounce. 'It's the light. The way it's hitting you there. You are without a doubt the most beautiful woman on earth!'

Tucka batted her eyes dreamily. Then she threw back her head and howled with laughter. She gasped for air. She pounded the table. 'You're really good!' she wheezed. 'I mean, you're even badder than I thought.'

'I try,' said Crounce with a devilish grin. He saluted her.

'At ease, soldier!' she told him. She dried her eyes with her napkin. Then she opened her menu and used it as a fan to shield them from their neighbours. 'So, what did you find out?'

'Just this,' said Crounce. He opened a large manila envelope and removed a document. He slid it across the table.

𝔓𝔯𝔬𝔪𝔦𝔰𝔰𝔬𝔯𝔶 𝔑𝔬𝔱𝔢

I promise to pay to the order of Nurella Pinch *(herein called the payee) the sum of* One Million *DOLLARS (*$1,000,000.00*), together with interest thereon at 6 per cent per annum from the date hereof until paid. To secure the payment of this note, the undersigned grants to the payee a security interest in the following collateral:*

THE VARMINT VARIETY THEATRE

together with all its contents, proceeds and products. If any payment due is not so paid, all principal and interest shall become immediately due to the holder of this note.

Signed, ***Fluster Varmint*** *Theatrical Impresario*

Crounce laid a small notebook on the table. 'According to this accounts ledger, Varmint only made two payments. And he hasn't paid a penny in over ten years. He still owes her $950,000.'

'Plus interest, surely,' mused Tucka.

Crounce nodded.

A rare look of peace and contentment filled Tucka's face. She reached again for her napkin. 'I'm just so touched,' she said, wiping her eyes. 'It's a very moving story.'

'You mean that Nurella would loan him a million dollars to buy the theatre?'

'No,' said Tucka. 'I mean that Varmint was so sentimental that he didn't destroy the loan papers when Nurella disappeared. The poor jerk! You'd never make a mistake like that, would you, dearest?'

'Never,' vowed Crounce. 'So, what do we do now?'

'Ruin him!' said Tucka blithely. 'And then take the theatre.' She reached for his hand. 'Isn't life grand? And this is only the beginning!'

'When I think of the possibilities!' said Crounce. 'Things I never dared to dream alone.'

'But now we're together! And there's a great big world out there waiting for us to come and get it.'

'Us!' said Crounce. 'I like the sound of that. I never thought I would.'

'I know. I waited so long to find someone. I'd given up. And then there you were. Smart. Shameless. Ruthless. And handsome. Everything I admire in a man.'

'You didn't mention greed.'

'Oh, greed,' said Tucka, savouring the sound of the word. 'That goes without saying.'

Hermux examined the tuft of wiry hair. 'I must have snagged it in the struggle. But look at this.' He held the hair out for Terfle to see. 'It's fake. I wonder who it belongs to? What do you think he was doing, sneaking around up there in the dark? And why did he try to kill me?'

Terfle shook her head.

'I'm sure the parrot knows what's going on. I've got to get back in there and get him to talk.'

There was a knock at the door, and Oaf looked in. 'Varmint wants to see you in his office right away!'

'I thought you said three o'clock?' said Hermux. 'I'm not quite ready.'

'Now,' said Oaf. 'And step on it. He's having a mood.'

With a sinking heart Hermux grabbed his empty sketchbook and prepared for the worst. But when he reached Varmint's office, he found that Varmint had forgotten all about the set and the production meeting.

'Things are bad!' he told Hermux. 'Read this! It just came.'

He handed Hermux a note.

Dear Fluster
(you lying cheating no-good louse),
     You didn't think you'd get away
with it, did you?
     You have until midnight tonight
to surrender the deed to the theatre.
     Or suffer the consequences!

                    a 'friend' of the family

'What do you think the consequences are?' asked Hermux.

An ear-shattering scream filled the air.

'Dad! Dad!'

'Beulith!' cried Varmint. 'That's Beulith!' He bolted from the office. Hermux followed.

They were met by a sickening sight. Beulith's motionless body lay crumpled at the foot of the stairs. For a mouse of his size Varmint could move surprisingly fast when it mattered. He descended the stairs in a single leap. He gathered his daughter into his arms.

'Beulith!' he sobbed. 'What happened?' He looked desperately at Hermux.

Beulith coughed. She pushed her father away and sat up.

'I think I'm OK,' she said. She straightened her blouse and dusted off her skirt. 'I must have tripped.'

Varmint helped her to her feet. 'You're sure no one pushed you?'

'Who would have pushed me? I was upset. That's all. I wasn't watching where I was going.' Beulith retrieved the afternoon newspaper from where it had fallen on the floor. 'But have you seen this?' She thrust the paper at her father. 'Please, Dad! Tell me she's lying!'

CITIZEN MERTSLIN EXPOSES VARMINT THEATRE SWINDLE!

Beauty tycoon launches a campaign to preserve superstar's legacy

A Moozella Corkin Exclusive

At a press conference this afternoon at Mertslin Cosmetics headquarters, CEO Tucka Mertslin announced the formation of an emergency legal fund to protect the estate of vanished film star Nurella Pinch.

'It's a disgrace!' Mertslin declared. 'She's our greatest star. She can't protect herself, and Fluster Varmint is robbing her blind!'

The legacy in question is Pinchester's historic Varmint Variety Theatre.

Secret documents proving Nurella Pinch the rightful owner of the Varmint Theater came to light recently during a routine cleaning at the theatre.

'Thanks to the courage of a civic-minded theatre worker, the spirit of Nurella Pinch can rest easy tonight,' said Mertslin. 'She may be dead. But she won't be forgotten. As soon as I am declared executor of the Nurella Pinch estate, we'll start eviction proceedings against Fluster Varmint and his ruthless band of theatre thieves.'

Meanwhile, Mertslin's plans to restore the theatre to the splendour of Nurella's era are moving along on schedule. She has already retained designer Rink Firsheen to oversee the renovation.

Tucka Mertslin's **Tartan Smile** *is now available at the beauty counter at Orsik & Arrbale.*

Hermux read the article over Varmint's shoulder.

'There's not a shred of truth to it. Is there?' Beulith prompted her father.

'Well, honey,' Varmint stalled, 'there are a few shreds. Here and there.'

'What?' Beulith wailed. 'Why didn't you tell me?'

'There wasn't that much to tell,' Varmint tried to explain. 'And she's got it all wrong, anyway.'

A small crowd of performers and crew gathered around them.

'What's happening?' asked the magician.

Hermux folded the paper and put it under his arm.

'Beulith took a spill,' he said. 'Let's get her upstairs. And get her some tea.'

Chapter 42
TROUBLE IN PARADISE

It was dark as usual in the Greasy Griddle. But not as dark as the expression on Corpius Crounce's face. He slapped the newspaper on the table in disgust. Through clenched teeth he said, 'I thought I was handling this.'

'But darling, you did handle it. Brilliantly. Then I handled it.' Tucka adjusted the shawl on her bare shoulders. Her fur had a summery glow. She had highlighted just the tips. 'Also brilliantly. It's a fabulous article. I couldn't have written it better myself.'

'What you've done is messed things up. Right now, publicity is the last thing we need.'

Tucka was shocked. It was the first stupid thing that Crounce had ever said to her. It hurt her to hear it.

'I had things all worked out,' Crounce grumbled. 'I've got Varmint figured out now. I know where he's vulnerable. Another day or two and he would have cracked. The theatre would have been ours and nobody the wiser.'

'But don't you see, dear? This way it will be legal,' Tucka argued. 'Things are so much simpler when they're legal. As soon as I control Nurella's estate, I'll sign the theatre over to myself. I mean to *us*! Then we'll be free to do whatever we want with it.'

'But you can't be her executor. You never even met her!'

'I did too. I saw her once at a premiere. She signed my autograph book. That meant a lot to me.' Tucka clenched her jaw ominously.

Crounce was outraged. 'So you think that some judge is going to declare you the legal executor of her estate? Just like that?'

'You're kidding, right?' Was it her imagination, or did Crounce seem a little smaller than she remembered?

'No, I'm not kidding!' he told her.

'Waitress!' Tucka bellowed.

A hamster in a hairnet shuffled over to their table.

'More coffee?' she asked blandly.

'Bring me a telephone!' Tucka ordered.

'Well, aren't we the princess!' cracked the waitress. 'This ain't the Swank and Swill, honey. There's a booth back by the kitchen.'

The booth, if anything, was darker than the restaurant. The glass was smudged. The door didn't close. And there were rude sayings scrawled all over the walls.

Tucka spritzed the telephone with a cleansing mist of *Lovely Like Me!* Then she dropped in a quarter and dialled.

'Judge Maudlin?' she trilled. She nodded at Crounce. 'It's Tucka calling! I'm so glad I caught you, you busy thing, you!' Tucka's voice dripped honey. 'And how are the re-election plans coming?' She listened for some time. 'Of course you have my support. When have you ever not had it?'

She toyed with Crounce's necktie.

'Me? Oh, you know! Work! Work! Work! Another day, another hundred thousand dollars! But I'm not calling about me. I'm doing community work now, and I'm going to need your help. You're still my little judgey-wudgey, aren't you?'

She pulled Crounce down close and blew in his ear.

'You're a dear. I knew I could count on you. It's Nurella Pinch. We've got to do something about her! Yes, she was fabulous! Absolutely my favourite too!'

Tucka traced a finger along Crounce's jaw.

'Well, the thing is that the poor dear went and died, and they never settled her estate properly. Nurella is part of our history. We've got to protect what little we have left to remember her by. If we don't do it now, it will be gone forever.'

She tickled Crounce's goatee.

'I knew you'd understand. Will it take long to appoint me executor? Thursday? That sounds lovely. Your courtroom or mine?' She laughed. 'Oh, I am wicked, aren't I? I'll see you Thursday morning!'

Tucka hung up the receiver.

'And that is how legitimate business works,' she said somewhat haughtily. 'But I guess you wouldn't know about that.'

'I stand corrected,' Crounce responded humbly.

'Apology accepted.' Talking to the judge had put Tucka in a forgiving mood. She squeezed Crounce's hand affectionately. 'The important thing is that together we make a perfect team.'

Walking back to their booth together hand in hand, the future seemed to stretch out before the two of them like an empty eight-lane highway that ran straight to their hearts' delights. Tucka had met her match at last. She would no longer be lonely at the top.

Chapter 43
REMEMBRANCE OF THINGS PAST

Varmint's wall safe was hidden behind the poster of the Okey-Dokey Girls. As Varmint dialled its combination, Hermux studied the poster. It was odd that all of their fates were suddenly tied up with the fate of Nurella Pinch, a woman he had never met. He studied her face. It was strangely familiar. But then how could it not be? Nurella Pinch had made more than a hundred films. There was something about her dance partner that seemed familiar as well. He was a handsome mouse with a perfect smile.

'Who's that with Nurella?' Hermux asked. 'Did he go into films too?'

Varmint stopped dialling a moment to look at the smiling mouse. He shook his head. 'I've got no idea,' he said. 'It was a long time ago.'

The safe opened.

'It should be right here.' He removed a stack of papers, set them on his desk, and began rifling through them. 'It's gone! It's impossible. I'm the only person with the combination.'

'The article says someone found them while they were cleaning,' observed Hermux. 'Who cleans in here?'

'Nobody cleans in here,' sniffed Beulith. 'Can't you tell? Dad

165

won't hear of it.'

'Now, now, Beulith! Don't be upset.'

'How can I not be upset? The newspaper just called us a bunch of thieves! You always told me we owned this theatre. You told me it was my future. I've worked my whole life for it. Now I find out that I've been working for some dead movie star. And they're going to take it away from us! Who's telling the truth?'

She looked from her father to Hermux. Then she exploded, 'And what are you doing here, anyway? This is family stuff! Why aren't you installing alarm clocks?' Beulith burst into tears.

Hermux didn't know what to say. He offered Beulith his handkerchief.

'I seem to have made a mess of everything,' Varmint said wearily. 'Both of you sit down, and I'll try to explain.

'Years ago Nurella Pinch and your mother were best friends. We were like a family.'

This was news to Beulith. 'What do you mean, a family?'

'We took care of each other. If she was in trouble, we helped her. If we were in trouble, she helped us.'

'What kind of trouble?' Beulith wanted to know.

'Financial trouble, for one. After you were born, a lot of things changed. Times were tough. Nurella left the company and went on to the movies. And your mother wanted us to settle down. She didn't want you growing up on the road. We found the theatre for sale, but we were broke. Nurella was already a star. She had the money. She wanted to give us the theatre. It was my idea to make it a loan. I guess it was pride.'

'She offered to give you a million dollars?' Beulith did not sound convinced.

'She was very rich.'

'That's still a lot of money.'

'Your mother was her closest friend, Beulith.'

'Then how come I never met her?'

'You did meet her. When you were little. You just don't remember.'

'And why didn't you pay her back?'

'I paid her some when I had it. But she didn't care about the money. She didn't need it. Then she had her accident, and your mother got sick. And everything just fell apart. I wasn't much good for anything. It was lucky for you that Glissin showed up.'

'But what about Nurella?'

'I never heard from her again. I tried to track her down, but she had disappeared. I assumed she was dead, like people said.'

'Apparently she is,' Beulith said gloomily. 'So we still owe her the money?'

'I don't know.' Varmint turned to Hermux. 'Don't just sit there, Tantamoq! Do something! That's what I'm paying you for.'

'It's really not his problem, Dad,' said Beulith. 'You hired Hermux to install alarm clocks.'

Hermux and Varmint exchanged uneasy glances.

'He is installing alarm clocks, isn't he?' Beulith asked. Her tone was sharp and pointed. 'What else is going on here?'

Chapter 44
Nuts!

Hermux rapped firmly on the door of Binter's dressing room. There was no answer. He set down his toolbox and got out his passkey. Then he let himself in and closed the door behind him without making a sound.

'Termind?' he whispered. 'Are you here?' He switched on the light.

The parrot's perch was empty. Below it lay the parrot, one wing spread awkwardly. Its outstretched claws seemed poised to ward off a blow. The parrot's head was twisted unnaturally to one side. Its beak was frozen open in what appeared to be a final death squawk.

'Termind! What did they do to you?' He ran to the parrot's side. Hermux delicately placed one paw on the parrot's chest. He could detect no movement. He gently raised the parrot's head. Its neck was unnervingly limp. As he peered anxiously at the feathered face, a malevolent, golden-ringed eye popped open.

'Daddy!' the parrot cried.

Hermux dropped its head and jumped backwards, tripping over his toolbox and tumbling on to the floor.

The parrot howled with laughter.

'Gotcha!' he snorted. He got to his feet and fluttered on to his perch. 'Look at you!' He flapped his wings in delight. 'Oh, Termind!' he mocked in Hermux's own voice. 'What did they do-o-o-o to you-u-u-u?'

Hermux got to his feet. He was not amused.

'I thought you were dead!'

'This is the most fun I've had in months! People are right. You really are funny!'

'What do you mean by that?'

'You know! Tucka Mertslin knocking you out with the Fizzy Bitters? I'm sorry I missed it.'

'What do you know about Tucka Mertslin?'

'Now it's Tucka, is it?' the parrot ruffled the feathers on its head into a loopy crown. He puffed out his chest. 'I know plenty! What did you bring me?'

Hermux opened his toolbox. He lifted up a family-size bag of roasted almonds and held it out for the parrot's inspection.

'Mmmm,' said the parrot, leaning forward eagerly. 'Salted?' he asked.

'You didn't say anything about salt!'

The parrot lunged for the almonds. But Hermux was faster.

'Oh, no, you don't!' he said. 'Not until you answer some questions.'

'All right,' the parrot agreed. 'Shoot!'

'First, who is Binter? And how does he know Tucka? And who got Nurella Pinch's mortgage papers out of the safe? And why does Tucka want the theatre? And what does she plan to do with it?'

'Whoa there, big mouse! You said a few questions. Not the history of the modern world!'

'OK, then let's begin with Binter. Who is he? And why is he here?'

The parrot gave in. 'I met him about six months ago. He's an ex –' The parrot stopped and looked warily at the door.

'An ex-what?'

There were footsteps outside.

'Hide!' said the parrot.

'Where?'

'In there! The closet!'

Two sliding doors concealed a shallow closet in the back wall of the dressing room. Hermux sprang towards them.

'The lights!' hissed the parrot.

Hermux spun around in midair. He ran to the door and snapped off the light switch.

A key rattled in the lock.

Hermux dashed for the closet again, and in the darkness he ran straight into his toolbox.

'Ow!' Hermux tried not to squeak. He fumbled in the darkness, grabbed the toolbox, and dragged it into the closet in a half limp, half hop. He slid the door closed and hid behind the rack of costumes.

The dressing-room lights came on again.

'Who were you talking to just now?' Binter asked suspiciously. 'I heard voices!'

'Nobody,' the parrot responded. 'I was just practising. Somebody in this act has got to practise.'

Binter was not satisfied. 'It sounded like a mouse's voice.'

'You mean like this?' the parrot asked. He cocked his head and assumed a very prim and proper posture. Then in a very mousy and singsong voice, he said, 'With a good alarm clock at our side, it is possible to face the most demanding schedule with absolute confidence, knowing that we will always be on time –'

Binter chuckled. 'You're really pretty good, you know!' he

said with grudging admiration.

'Then give me a raise!' quipped the parrot.

'Over my dead body!' said Binter. 'Hey! Has Tantamoq been snooping around here again?'

'Haven't seen him.'

'Then whose are these?' Binter stooped and picked up the bag of almonds from the floor.

Hermux flattened himself against the wall of the closet.

'They belong to your apprentice, Magner Wooliun,' said the parrot without a blink. 'Or whatever he's calling himself today.'

The ventriloquist ripped open the bag and stuffed a handful of almonds into his mouth. 'We don't need to mention this to Magner,' he said.

'And I won't mention it to his girlfriend either. They were a gift from Tucka.' The parrot spoke in Tucka's breathiest whisper.

'I don't like her,' said Binter.

'And she doesn't like you. You lack style. I'm more her type.'

'You know, you're starting to get on my nerves!' said Binter with his mouth still full. 'Now shut up and keep still. We gotta go get fitted for new costumes.'

Carrying the parrot's perch, Binter shut off the lights and left, locking the door behind him. Moments later, Hermux crept out of the closet. His head was spinning with new information.

'So he's Tucka's boyfriend,' he thought. 'Wait a minute! That doesn't make sense. Why is she dating a ventriloquist's apprentice? Unless maybe he's not really a ventriloquist's apprentice at all. But then who is he really? Is it he and Tucka who've been threatening Varmint? And what do they want with the theatre, anyway?' It was very confusing. Hermux needed more time alone with the parrot. He quietly let himself out of the dressing room and sneaked back downstairs.

'At least this time nobody saw me,' he congratulated himself.

Unfortunately, he was wrong. Concealed in the shadows of the stage, someone had been watching Hermux with great interest. It was someone who also wanted some time alone with the parrot.

Chapter 45
THE BURDEN OF PROOF

On the worktable the teacups rattled in their saucers. Terfle, who was positioning sequins on a glittering new cape for the hypnotist, stopped her work and looked up at the ceiling.

'They're finishing "The Can-Can",' Glissin said. She knotted a sequin in place and bit off the thread. 'It sounds like a good audience tonight.'

It was. Tucka's accusations had created a scandal. That night's performance at the Varmint was sold out.

'Hermux?' Glissin asked.

'Yes?' He closed his sketchbook and put down his pencil.

'She can't do it, can she? Tucka Mertslin? She can't take over the theatre like that.'

'Tucka is used to doing whatever she wants,' said Hermux, who was feeling a bit discouraged. He hadn't made any more progress towards solving the case. Or designing the set except for writing his name and telephone number inside his sketchbook.

'But it can't be legal! Nurella's not dead.'

'She's not?' asked Hermux. He put down the alarm clock he was wiring and looked at her with interest. 'How do you know?'

'I mean, it's never been proved, has it? Don't they need proof?'

'I don't know,' said Hermux. 'She's been gone for a long time. Even her husband can't find her. And he's been looking for years!'

'What husband?' The sequin Glissin was sewing slipped from her fingers and vanished on the floor.

'Brinx Lotelle,' said Hermux. 'The film director.'

'Brinx!' said Glissin icily. 'You mean her *ex*-husband. They haven't been married for years.'

'I'm sorry,' said Hermux. 'Her *ex*-husband. What difference does it make? He still can't find her.'

'Is he looking?'

'He's making a movie,' Hermux explained. 'The story of Nurella Pinch. Even though she dumped him, he still loves her.'

'Ouch!' said Glissin. She had pricked herself with her sewing needle.

'Did you know Nurella?' Hermux asked. 'I never thought to ask you.'

Glissin rubbed her finger thoughtfully.

'Not really well,' she said. 'I worked with her on a couple of films. But I knew her well enough to know that Brinx Lotelle married her for his career, and then dumped her the minute he thought she was no longer useful.'

'Oh,' said Hermux, embarrassed.

'You know that after her accident Brinx never set foot in the hospital. He never visited her even once.'

'You're kidding!' Hermux was secretly pleased to know that Brinx was a liar and a cad, just as he had thought.

Glissin stood up suddenly. 'Is that what your friend Linka is working on? Brinx's movie?'

'Yes,' said Hermux.

'Just the two of them?'

'He wanted to keep it small. So he could move fast. That's what he told Linka.'

'I'm sure he did.'

'What do you mean?' asked Hermux. He was getting a bad feeling.

'Brinx always moves fast. That's why he calls himself an *action* film director. Next he'll be asking her to do a screen test.'

'He already asked,' said Hermux.

'I'm sorry to hear that,' said Glissin. 'What did she say?'

But Hermux didn't get to answer. Overhead there was a horrifying crash, followed by muffled screams and the sounds of running feet.

Chapter 46
IN THE SPOTLIGHT

When Hermux and Glissin arrived on the stage, the curtain was down. The orchestra had stopped playing. A crowd had gathered at one side.

'My baby!' wailed a familiar voice. It was Varmint.

Glissin pushed her way through the crowd.

'What happened?' she asked. 'What happened?'

'It's Beulith! An accident!' the magician told her. He stepped back to let her by.

Glissin couldn't believe her eyes. There on the floor lay the shattered remains of a giant spotlight. Unharmed next to it sat Beulith.

'You're OK?' asked Glissin, kneeling beside her.

Beulith nodded. In fact, she appeared unshaken. It was her father who was hysterical.

'An inch closer and you would have been killed –' Varmint babbled.

'Dad! I'm OK!' Beulith assured him. 'It was just an accident.' She got to her feet, helped her father up, and shooed the crowd away. 'Let's get on with the show, folks!'

As the performers returned to their places, Glissin rejoined Hermux.

'An odd accident,' she said. 'I've never seen a light like that fall in all my years in the theatre.'

'More than odd,' said Hermux. He scanned the stage, looking for the ventriloquist and his apprentice. He spotted them standing in the wings, their faces partially obscured in shadow. Was it a trick of the light, or were they smiling as they watched Beulith and her father leave the stage? As Hermux looked harder, he saw the parrot between them, seated on its perch. The parrot saw him watching and ever so slightly nodded its head.

'What do you know about the ventriloquist?' Hermux asked Glissin under his breath.

'Not much. He's pretty new to the show. He keeps to himself, mostly.'

'And what about his apprentice?'

'He's a strange one,' she said. 'He looks harmless, but I'm not sure I trust him.'

'Me neither,' said Hermux.

On their way home from the theatre that night, neither Hermux nor Terfle said a word. Terfle was tired. Her forelegs ached from pushing sequins all day, and her eyes felt permanently dazzled from all the glitter and shine. Hermux was tired too. It had been an exhausting day. Too much had happened in too short a time. None of it good. And Hermux was worried. He hardly knew who or what to worry about first.

When he found a postcard from Linka in his mailbox, it seemed like a sign. He decided that he would worry about Linka the entire evening and try to forget all about Varmint and Beulith and the others until tomorrow. It seemed like an excellent plan until he looked at the postcard.

On it was a portrait of Nurella Pinch.

Hermux propped the card up on his desk and stared at it. It was a glamorous photograph taken at the peak of her fame. The pretty young mouse from the Okey-Dokey Girls had grown into an exquisitely beautiful woman with luscious, thick fur. Her eyelashes and whiskers, coal black and impossibly long, cast dramatic shadows across her face. Nurella Pinch was born for the camera, but she remained slightly beyond its reach. She seemed to shimmer like someone from a dream – painfully familiar and yet unrecognizable.

Hermux felt curiously moved.

'I guess that's what made her such a star,' he told Terfle, who seemed equally taken by Nurella's image. 'We all think that we know her. But I'll bet that no one really knew her. Certainly not Brinx Lotelle.'

Terfle bristled at the sound of Brinx's name.

'I'm sorry I even brought him up,' said Hermux. 'But I can't stop thinking about him. I can't stop thinking about any of them. Nurella and Tucka and Beulith and Varmint and the parrot and the theatre! It's too much! It's like putting together a clock with five hands and two main springs. I can't figure out how they all fit together. Or if they do fit together!'

Terfle nodded sympathetically.

'I don't know about you,' said Hermux. 'But I'm exhausted. I'm going to bed.'

He was brushing his teeth when the phone rang.

It was Linka.

'Is it too late to be calling?' she asked.

'No!' said Hermux. He mopped toothpaste drool from his chin. 'Where are you?'

'We're in Dranton,' said Linka. 'Where Nurella grew up. It's been quite a day!'

'It was quite a day here too,' said Hermux. 'What happened?'

'We spent the morning filming Nurella's childhood home. It's abandoned now and pretty creepy and rundown. Brinx loved that, of course. Then we drove out to the nursing home and interviewed Nurella's fourth-grade teacher. Her name is Mrs Thiggin. She gave Nurella her first part in a play. A school production of *The Runaway Squirrel*. Nurella won the award for best actress. They gave her a watch as a prize. It had two little masks on it for comedy and tragedy. It sounded so sweet.'

'That does sound nice,' said Hermux. 'I don't think I've ever seen a watch like that.'

'What's happening at the theatre?' asked Linka.

Hermux tried to explain everything that had taken place that day.

'I'm completely confused,' said Linka.

'So am I. But I'm going to talk to the parrot again tomorrow.' Hermux cleared his throat. 'You didn't say how your screen test went. Are you going to be a movie star?'

There was dead silence.

'Linka? Are you still there?'

'I'm here.'

'Well? How was it?' Hermux prepared himself for bad news.

'It's a long story,' she said. 'Why don't we talk about it when I get home?'

Chapter 48
MESMERIZING PERFORMANCE

For the second time that year, the doughnut-maker at Lanayda's was broken. Hermux ordered maple-seed pancakes. Nip had oatmeal.

'Sounds like everything at the shop is fine,' said Hermux. 'I wish I could say the same thing about the theatre.'

'What's happened now?' asked Nip.

Hermux told him.

'Who would want to hurt Beulith?' Nip pounded the table angrily and nearly upset their coffees.

'I think I know,' said Hermux. 'But I need some proof. Do you think a parrot can testify in court?'

'Not sure. It depends on the judge.'

'Well, right now the parrot is my best bet.'

Nip's attention was drawn to a stylish young gerbil in the booth next to them. She had a golden cricket on a leash and was feeding it crumbs from her plate.

Hermux turned to see. 'That reminds me. I've got to stop on the way to the theatre and buy more almonds.'

'What for?' asked Nip.

'Bribing the witness. And I've got to figure out how to get in to see him again without getting caught.'

A tiny light flashed in the Port-a-Pet Palace. Nip tapped Hermux's wrist.

'Look at that!' he whispered. He pointed down at Terfle. 'I think she's hypnotizing that cricket.'

Hermux and Nip leaned closer and watched in fascination as Terfle, standing at the door of her cage, used a turquoise sequin to focus a beam of light at the cricket. She waved it back and forth. Seated next to its mistress, the cricket had stopped eating. It bulbous eyes stared vacantly towards the Port-a-Pet. Terfle waved a free leg, and the cricket suddenly fell over on its side.

'Dinky!' the stylish gerbil shrieked. 'What's wrong?' She grabbed her glass of water and doused the cricket. It sat up, coughing and sputtering. She clutched it to her protectively. 'My poor baby!' she cooed, stroking its glossy head. 'My poor, poor baby! Dinky needs fresh air! Let's get you out of here!' As she carried the cricket out the door, it gazed back inquisitively over her shoulder, as though awaiting further instructions from Terfle.

When they were gone, Hermux scolded, 'That wasn't very nice, Terfle! You scared that lady. And who knows what you did to that cricket.'

Terfle put down her sequin and hung her head in shame.

'She's been learning a lot of new things at the theatre,' Hermux explained to Nip. 'She can do card tricks too.'

'I'd like to see that!' said Nip.

'Maybe next time.' Hermux ate the last bite of pancake and finished his coffee. 'We've got to get going. I have a feeling it's going to be a big day.'

As Hermux and Terfle approached the theatre, that feeling only got stronger. Parked in front of the stage door were two police cars with red lights flashing.

Chapter 49
KIDNAPPED!

'What's going on?' Hermux asked the old door gopher.

'There's been a kidnapping,' the gopher said. 'The police just got here.'

'Oh my gosh! It must be Beulith!' Terfle struggled to stay on her perch as Hermux raced inside, swinging the Port-a-Pet wildly as he ran. The stage lights were up full. And loud voices could be heard at the back. The sounds led straight to Gilden Binter's dressing room.

It was crowded with people. Standing on his toes, Hermux could make out the ventriloquist's figure slumped against the parrot's perch. Next to Binter stood a stout police rat.

'Now, hold it there just one minute!' the police rat said. 'Let me get this straight. You telling me that this missing parrot is a dummy?'

'An irreplaceable dummy!' Binter howled in protest.

'I don't care if he's the greatest dummy on earth! It's not kidnapping!' the police rat said angrily. 'It's theft! And it's not even grand theft. You dragged me out of headquarters for that? I ought to run you in for making a false alarm.'

Hermux recognized the police rat's voice. He hadn't been

very helpful to Hermux when Linka was kidnapped by Dr Mennus. Hermux instinctively drew back into the crowd. But not before the ventriloquist spotted him. He jumped to his feet.

'Why don't you ask Tantamoq?' Binter pointed an accusing claw at Hermux. 'He was snooping around in here just the other day!'

'Tantamoq?' The police rat scratched his head. 'Why does that name sound familiar?'

At that moment Binter's apprentice arrived.

'What's happening?' he asked.

Binter told him.

'Officer,' the apprentice said suavely. 'I'm afraid this is all a big mistake. It's my fault.'

'And who are you?'

'I'm Mr Binter's apprentice,' he said. 'My name is Magner Wooliun.'

Hermux was struck by how easily the apprentice seemed to take charge of the situation.

'Mr Binter has been under a lot of pressure this week, getting ready for the big new show,' the apprentice went on. Hermux noticed that he looked directly at Binter as he spoke, as though warning him not to contradict him. 'I told you yesterday that I was taking the dummy home to clean it.'

'You did not,' said Binter. 'I would remember that. Where is he?'

'Still drying,' said Magner. 'He'll be ready this afternoon.'

'This guy is a smooth operator,' thought Hermux. 'And he's no apprentice, that's for sure. He acts like he's the boss.'

'Still drying!' cried Binter. 'You can't wash a dummy like that. I'm ruined!'

'Nonsense,' said Magner. He gave the policeman a glib smile.

'We wash dummies all the time. Gentle cycle. No bleach. Believe me, he looks better than new.'

Watching him, Hermux felt a shock of recognition. 'That smile!' he thought. 'I've seen it somewhere recently. But where? And look at those ears! They've got hair sprouting out of them. He's the guy who nearly killed me upstairs!' Hermux had a bad feeling that the parrot was in trouble. He considered telling the police rat what he knew. But who would believe him? A parrot pretending to be a dummy for a shrew pretending to be ventriloquist? With Tucka Mertslin's boyfriend pretending to be his apprentice?

Before he could decide what to do, Beulith burst into the dressing room.

'Hermux!' she said, wide-eyed and frantic. 'Thank goodness you're here! Dad needs you out front! Right now!'

Chapter 50
OPERATION DIGNITY

Tucka Mertslin had commandeered the lobby of the theatre. She had arrived with an entourage that included Rink Firsheen, Moozella Corkin, reporters and photographers from the *Weekly Squeak*, His Righteous Honour Chief Judge Jiggery Maudlin, and a bus full of employees from Tucka Mertslin Cosmetics. Tucka was there to hold a press conference.

'Why don't you throw her out?' Hermux asked Varmint, who had taken refuge in the ticket booth with Oaf the hedgehog and Glissin.

'I tried,' answered Varmint. 'But we're outnumbered!'

Tucka tapped a microphone. 'Everybody quiet down!' she said. The lobby grew silent. Tucka took a deep breath. 'First, I want to thank all of you for coming out this morning to support the preservation of our cultural heritage *and* to fight for justice in our community!'

'Justice now!' her employees chanted. 'Justice now!'

'Don't worry, my friends,' she intoned. 'I am with you. And justice will be ours!' She nodded benevolently at Judge Maudlin.

'But before we begin our historic struggle,' Tucka continued, 'I've brought you here to see what we are fighting for.' Behind

Tucka stood an enormous easel covered with a dark cloth. At her signal, Rink pulled the cloth away and revealed a full-colour rendering of Tucka Mertslin's Majestic Theatre.

Rink pointed out the new and improved features of the theatre block, which included all new shops.

The 'I Dream of Tucka' Fashion Boutique

Tucka at Home

Tucka's Bed and Bath

Tucka in the Kitchen

Tucka's Garden Shop

Gifts by Tucka

Flowers by Tucka

Tucka's Bridal Suite

and

Tucka for Tots

'Welcome to a Totally Tucka World!' crowed Rink.

'Ka-ching!' shouted Tucka's employees.

'Ka-ching!' Tucka shouted back.

The reaction in the ticket booth was more subdued.

'I thought it was going to be Nurella Pinch's theatre,' Glissin sniffed.

'Apparently not,' commented Beulith. 'She's got a lot of nerve!'

'Nerves of steel,' said Hermux, speaking from experience.

'Well, she won't get away with it!' said Glissin with uncharacteristic vigour. 'We'll stop her!'

'How?' asked Beulith.

Glissin looked around desperately. Her eyes fell on Hermux. 'Hermux will manage!' She pushed him out the door. 'Do something!' she implored.

Tucka had opened the floor to questions.

'Miss Mertslin, is it true that a portion of the profits from the stores will be donated to charity?'

'I'm glad you asked that,' said Tucka. 'And the answer is yes. Part of every dollar you spend will go to support the Tucka Mertslin Foundation for the Promotion of Beauty in its vital missionary work. Are there any more questions?'

Hermux raised his hand. Tucka ignored him.

'I guess not,' she said. 'In that case, I want to thank all of you for coming today –'

'I have a question!' Hermux shouted.

'Well, what is it?' asked Tucka.

'I thought you said you were doing this for Nurella Pinch.' Hermux's voice trembled with indignation. 'I don't see any mention of her anywhere!'

The crowd held its breath.

'That's not a question,' said Tucka primly. 'That's a comment. And we don't have time for comments!'

'All right,' said Hermux. 'What does any of this have to do with Nurella Pinch?'

'What does it have to do with Nurella Pinch? That's a fine question coming from you! What could you possibly know about Nurella Pinch? Have you any idea what it's like to be a legend in your own time? To be a household name? I don't think so. But I do. I know only too well. I ask myself, what would I want if I were in Nurella's place today? And I can tell you right now, I wouldn't want anything vain or grand.'

Tucka held out her hand.

'Rink, give me the magnifying glass!' Rink passed her a large magnifying glass. Tucka held it up in front of the rendering of the theatre. Above the fire hydrant, between the stage door and the trash cans, was a minuscule brass plaque. Tucka squinted to read it. 'In memory of Nurella Pinch.'

Her employees clapped wildly. During the commotion, no one but Tucka noticed the handsome and debonair mouse who suddenly appeared on the stairs to the balcony. He stopped halfway down, stroking his goatee as he watched the scene below.

'Believe me,' she said. 'This is exactly what Nurella would want.'

Tucka raised her arms for silence.

'Let us close our eyes and summon the spirit of the dearly departed. Nurella Pinch? Nurella?'

'I think I'm going to be sick,' Glissin whispered to Hermux.

'I already am,' said Hermux.

'Nurella!' intoned Tucka. 'Wherever you are, if you can hear me, give me a sign.'

The mouse on the stairs rapped the banister three times.

'I knew it,' Tucka crowed. 'I feel her presence. And she is happy. Nurella is happy at last.'

At her words, a scattering of hand-painted signs rose above the audience.

NURELLA PINCH
Happy at last!

Tucka tapped the microphone. 'It's too soon to celebrate yet. We still have a legal battle before us. But Judge Maudlin is here with us today. And I think he has some words of encouragement.'

Tucka gave the judge the microphone, and he gave her a little pinch.

'Don't worry, folks,' he said cheerily. 'The law is on our side. We'll get all the legal details cleared up tomorrow morning. Ten a.m. at the courthouse. Be there, or be square!'

Chapter 51

THE SHOW MUST GO ON

'Well?' asked Varmint. 'What do you think? I want to print it for tomorrow morning.' On his desk was a drawing for a poster announcing the *Silver Jubilee Spectacular*.

'It looks nice,' said Hermux, trying to sound enthusiastic.

'Stop it!' cried Beulith. 'Both of you! Just stop it! Please!'

'What's wrong?' asked Varmint. 'Do you think the type's too small?'

'How can you even think about posters? Remember? Tucka Mertslin?' Beulith cried. 'We're going to be thrown out on the street!'

'No, we won't,' said Varmint. 'Hermux is taking care of that. Aren't you?' He elbowed Hermux in the side.

Hermux gulped.

'You let him handle it, honey. Hermux has got the whole situation under control. Our job is to stay focused on the opportunity!'

'The opportunity to start all over?' asked Beulith.

'If it comes to that,' answered Varmint. He sounded determined. Then his face stretched into a rubbery grin. 'But it won't! And in the meantime we've got tickets to sell. There's going to be a huge crowd at the courthouse tomorrow. And I want every person there to go home with a poster. We're not done yet!'

He put a heavy arm around each of them and spoke in his inspirational voice.

'We've got a show to do! And we're going to do it! And Tantamoq, this means you too! Stop messing around with those stupid alarm clocks for now and get me a stage design! I need it yesterday!'

He walked them briskly to the door.

'Now, both of you, cheer up! And get to work!'

When they were gone, Varmint closed the door and locked it. Then he collapsed against it and sank slowly to the floor.

'What are we going to do?' he sighed. 'What in the world are we going to do?'

Chapter 52
WATCH IT!

Glissin had wanted to talk to Hermux. But before he went downstairs, Hermux paid a visit to Binter's dressing room. He knocked, and when there was no response, he let himself in and switched on the lights.

The parrot was back.

'Thank goodness!' said Hermux. 'I was worried about you.'

The parrot stared at him without speaking.

'No games,' said Hermux. 'I need to know what they're planning next.'

The parrot said nothing.

Hermux found himself getting angry.

'I'm tired of playing around! People could get hurt. *You* could get hurt! I need some evidence to stop them! Anything!' He poked the parrot in the chest for emphasis.

'I'm not falling for this again!'

The parrot didn't move.

A sickening feeling came over Hermux. He poked the parrot again. More gently this time. A trickle of sawdust fell from beneath one wing.

Termind, the parrot of a thousand voices, had been stuffed.

Hermux got out of there fast. Walking as steadily as he could, he headed straight for Glissin's studio. Glissin and Terfle knew that something was terribly wrong as soon as he came in.

'What's happened?' asked Glissin.

He told them.

'It's my fault,' he said when he had finished. 'He'd still be alive if it weren't for me.'

'No,' said Glissin. 'He'd still be alive if it weren't for whoever killed him.'

Terfle agreed.

'Either way, he's still dead,' said Hermux. 'I feel terrible. I can't even prove he was ever alive. And we're no closer to stopping Tucka than before.'

Glissin refilled their teacups.

'What did you want to talk to me about?' Hermux asked. 'It sounded important.'

'The court hearing tomorrow –'

'Tomorrow morning!' Hermux burst out. 'And now Varmint is pressuring me about designing the set! I think Beulith may be right. He may be losing his mind.'

'We're all feeling the pressure,' said Glissin. Indeed, there was a slight tremble in her paw as she poured. 'Sugar?'

'Two,' said Hermux. He didn't care about calories. He was trying to avert a disaster, and it seemed as though he was doomed to fail. This time tomorrow, it could all be over. He watched Glissin spoon the sugar. 'That's an interesting watch you've got. I've never seen you wear it before.'

She dropped the spoon, spraying sugar across the worktable.

'I'm so clumsy today,' she said. 'Pins and needles.'

'May I see it?' asked Hermux.

'It's just a trinket,' she said. 'It hardly keeps time any more.'

Somewhat reluctantly Glissin extended her arm. On her wrist was a gold watch. It was nicked and scratched and framed by two masks – one smiling, one frowning.

'I could fix it for you,' offered Hermux.

'Oh, no,' said Glissin. 'It's too much bother.'

'It's no bother,' said Hermux.

He stared at the watch. 'It's just like the one they gave Nurella Pinch when she was a little girl,' he thought. 'That's an odd coincidence.' Hermux tried to remember what Varmint had told him about Glissin. She showed up at the theatre when Varmint's wife got sick. That would have been about the same time that Nurella Pinch disappeared. And Nurella Pinch was Varmint's wife's best friend. In fact, Glissin had been here the entire time that Nurella had been missing. 'That's an even odder coincidence,' thought Hermux. He looked at Glissin in a new light.

Hermux tried to picture her with glamorous lighting and luscious, thick fur. He tried to imagine her with impossibly long coal-black eyelashes and arching whiskers. And a smouldering look in her eyes. 'No!' he told himself. 'That would take some amazing acting!' Then he stopped himself. 'What am I saying? That's exactly what Nurella Pinch was! A great actress!' Hermux almost spilled hot tea all over his lap.

'Your watch was a gift, wasn't it?' he asked impulsively.

'Yes, it was,' answered Glissin. 'How did you know?'

'Mrs Thiggin still talks about giving it to you.'

'Mrs Thiggin?' Glissin's face was a picture of innocence. 'I'm afraid I –'

'*The Runaway Squirrel*,' said Hermux. He watched her closely. 'You won the award for best actress, I think. You would never deserve anything less.'

Hermux had never spoken to a movie star before. Much less the greatest star of all time. He had no earthly idea what he should say to Nurella Pinch.

It was uncomfortably quiet.

'This is really good tea,' he said awkwardly.

Glissin didn't seem to hear him. She looked around the costume shop. Her eyes took in the mannequins, the sewing machines, and the unfinished sketches as though committing each detail to memory. Finally she returned her attention to Hermux. 'I knew I couldn't hide forever,' she said sadly. 'But it's hard to let it go.'

'But you don't have to!' said Hermux. 'You own it.'

'Nurella owns it,' said Glissin. 'Not me.'

'But *you're* Nurella Pinch!'

'I can't be Nurella *and* Glissin.'

'Well, then, stop being Glissin!' Hermux yelled.

There was a sharp jingle from the Port-a-Pet Palace. Terfle was ringing the emergency bell.

'I'm sorry!' apologized Hermux. 'You're right. That was rude.' He sat down again. 'Maybe you could explain,' he said politely. 'Why can't you just be Nurella again?'

'I don't want to be Nurella again,' said Glissin.

'But she's famous!'

'I know.'

'I don't understand,' said Hermux.

'I'll try to explain it. I worked very hard to create Nurella. I gave her my whole life. And what did I get back?'

'I don't know.'

'I don't know either, Hermux. I didn't get friends. I didn't get love. I got money. But then I had my "accident" with Dr Mennus. You know about that, don't you?'

Hermux nodded.

'It was a terrible time. My career ended overnight. Brinx left me. I had a breakdown. I ran out of money. And then things got worse. Beulith's mother got sick. She called me. She was dying. My best friend in the world. Dying. And she had a daughter. She asked me –' Glissin sobbed.

'I'm so sorry,' said Hermux.

'She asked me to watch out for Beulith. And that's what I've done. She saved my life!' said Glissin fiercely. 'Do you understand? It was my chance to escape from being Nurella. To start a new life. A good life.'

'I think I do. But what if Varmint tells them you're here?'

'Varmint?' she asked. 'He may be a great producer, but he can't see a foot beyond the footlights. He has no idea who I am.'

'Then you have to tell him. And tell the others too. Tell Tucka! Before it's too late!'

'As much as I would like to,' she said, 'I can't.'

'What do you mean, you can't?'

'Nurella Pinch is gone. She was a character I played.'

'But you're an actress.'

Glissin smiled. 'I am, aren't I? Sometimes I forget that.' She looked around her studio. 'You know, I love this place, Hermux. At first it was just my hiding place. Nurella had to disappear, and who would ever think of looking for her here in the basement? And Glissin. Quiet, hardworking Glissin. Believe me, I couldn't have found a better disguise for Nurella Pinch. I thought I would get bored with her, but I was wrong. She's a very interesting character.'

'Everyone likes Glissin.'

'I like Glissin too. And that's not something I could say about Nurella.'

'But couldn't you be Nurella again? And do something to save the theatre?'

Glissin tapped her foot nervously. 'I can't be Nurella *and* Glissin. And I'm not ready for Glissin's story to end. I'm not just acting any more. I'm living.'

'But what about Varmint's story? And Beulith's? And the theatre's? Don't they matter?'

'Of course they do!' Glissin fought back tears. 'They're all that matters. Don't you see? Glissin has a purpose. She's got a reason to live. Nurella didn't. She still doesn't!'

Hermux looked at Terfle. She raised her feelers hopefully.

'Maybe she could find one,' said Hermux.

Chapter 54
DRESSED TO KILL

'Mirror, mirror, in the hall, in four-inch heels I look quite tall,' Tucka sang contentedly.

And she did look tall. She looked tall, stately and graceful in black silk crepe.

She draped a mourning veil over her face and tried to look sad. It wasn't easy after all the excitement of the day. She was practically the owner of a world-renowned theatre.

She considered the veil. Maybe it was too much to wear in a courtroom. But grief was definitely the right look. After all, in a way, it was Nurella's funeral.

'Still, I hate the way it hides my eyes.' She slipped it off and with a few snips of her scissors, she cut two large almond-shaped holes for her eyes. When she put the veil back on, she was quite pleased.

She blew herself a kiss.

'Nobody is as much fun as you,' she told herself. In the mirror her reflection agreed completely. They got along together perfectly. They always had. Never a cross word. Never a moment of jealousy. It was a wonderful relationship. If only her relationship with Crounce turned out to be half as exciting, she would be content.

Tucka threw the veil aside. She went into the kitchen, opened the walk-in freezer, and chose a small tub of chocolate-fudgey-mocha ice cream. She grabbed a tablespoon from the drawer and wandered into the living room. Stationed in front of Rink's model of Mertslin's Majestic Theatre, she emptied her mind of all distractions.

'Mine, mine, mine,' she chanted between scoops of ice cream. As she spoke the words, a feeling of pure bliss enveloped her. It was very nice. In fact, she had never felt like it before. It was a feeling she had to share with someone.

Tucka reached for the telephone and dialled a number she knew by heart. The line rang through.

'Moozella?' crooned Tucka. 'It's me. About tomorrow morning! We've got to talk.'

Chapter 55

OPEN AND SHUT CASE

Anxious to make a good impression, Hermux got up early and dressed carefully for his first day in court. He wore a bright yellow shirt, his orange daisy necktie, his pink-and-red plaid vest, and his blue corduroy suit with brass buttons. Terfle waxed her shell and polished her feet. She wanted to look her best too.

They were the first to arrive in court. Hermux took a seat in the front of the courtroom. He placed his briefcase on the table in front of him. Nip followed, carrying the Port-a-Pet. He placed it next to Hermux's briefcase so Terfle could have a good view of the proceedings. Hermux opened his briefcase and showed the contents to Nip. Inside there were two carefully wrapped celery doughnuts. He closed the briefcase.

'We're ready,' he told Terfle and Nip. 'Now all we can do is hope.'

The room began to fill up fast. Moozella Corkin took a seat in the first row. Rink Firsheen sat next to her. The Pinchester branch of the Nurella Pinch Fan Club occupied a whole section. Tucka's employees took up another. The chorus squirrels from the Varmint another. Varmint and Beulith arrived and joined

Hermux, Nip and Terfle at the front table. Beulith had clearly been crying.

'Have you seen Glissin?' she asked Hermux. 'I was sure she'd be here.'

'No,' said Hermux. 'I haven't. She might be in the balcony.'

Nip got up immediately. 'Should I go look for her?' he asked. 'I'd be happy to do it. Do you want me to give her a message?'

'No,' said Beulith. 'I was just wondering.'

'Don't worry,' he assured her. 'Hermux has prepared a very strong case.'

At that moment Tucka arrived. She wore her veil and carried a gargantuan bunch of long-stemmed white lilies. As she walked solemnly down the aisle, she handed out the lilies along with buttons that read:

Memories
The tribute fragrance
from
Tucka Mertslin
(scratch here and sniff)

When she reached the front of the courtroom, Tucka took her place at the table opposite Hermux and the Varmints. She lifted her veil with a grand gesture and dropped it to the floor. She set a small, framed photo of Nurella Pinch on the table, placed a votive candle before it, lit the candle, and stood for a moment. She closed her eyes and bowed her head. Then, in a stage whisper that could be clearly heard in the last row of the balcony, she said, 'It's going to be OK, Nurella! You're in good hands now!'

The door to Judge Maudlin's private chambers opened. His clerk, a gopher in wireframed glasses, appeared.

'All rise for Judge Maudlin!'

Judge Jiggery Maudlin was a woodchuck of some distinction. He swept into court like a man who was used to having his own way. He seated himself with great ceremony, then banged his gavel and announced, 'I will not tolerate any nonsense in my courtroom.' He glared at Hermux and the Varmints. Then he turned to Tucka.

'Miss Mertslin!' he said, baring an impressive pair of front teeth. 'You look positively ravishing this morning.'

'Your Honour,' chided Tucka. 'Behave yourself! I expect a fair and impartial hearing. Nothing less!'

Judge Maudlin scratched at the air with one paw and growled. Then he got serious. 'And who are you?' he asked Hermux brusquely.

Hermux rose to his feet.

'I'm Hermux Tantamoq. I'm here on behalf of the Varmint Variety Theatre.' Hermux indicated Fluster and Beulith.

Judge Maudlin stared at them blankly.

'The crooks, Your Honour,' Tucka said helpfully.

'Oh, right!' he said. 'Sit down!' he told Hermux.

Hermux sat down. He felt his confidence beginning to wane.

'Your Honour,' Tucka continued. 'I think I can save us a lot of time. It's a very simple case, really. Nurella Pinch was a great actress and a great beauty. When her beauty was destroyed in a

203

tragic accident, she withdrew from public view. Then she suffered a complete mental breakdown. And shortly after that she vanished. She has never been seen again. As the world's foremost authority on every aspect of beauty, it is my expert opinion that Miss Pinch was driven by grief and shame over the loss of her beauty to take her own life. As her dear friend and as a friend of Pinchester, I ask the court to declare Nurella Pinch officially dead and to appoint me executor of her estate.'

'Sounds OK to me,' said Judge Maudlin. 'And are there any objections?'

Hermux jumped to his feet. 'Your Honour!'

'What do you want?' demanded the judge.

Hermux looked at the judge. Judge Maudlin looked at his watch. He waited.

'Say something!' grunted Varmint.

Hermux looked at Tucka. She glared back icily.

'Your Honour,' Hermux began feebly, 'I'm afraid that – '

Terfle's emergency bell rang loud and clear.

Hermux looked back at the door.

There she stood, framed in the doorway, wearing a beautifully tailored red suit and a broad-brimmed black hat. She looked older than her pictures. But it was unmistakably her.

'Your Honour!' said Hermux in a voice that rang with relief, 'I would like to call a witness. I would like to call Miss Nurella Pinch!'

Chapter 56

IDENTITY CRISIS

'And do you solemnly swear to tell the truth, the whole truth, and no hokum, blarney or baloney?'

'I do.'

'You may be seated.'

Nurella sat down. From the witness box she could see the entire courtroom. She registered the relief in Hermux's eyes and the shock on Varmint's face. Beulith was harder to read. Was it gratitude? Was it wonder at seeing her mother's best friend? Or was there a glimmer of recognition in her eyes? She couldn't think about it now. She had a performance to do. And with Tucka in the front row, she knew it was going to be a tough audience.

Draped in black from head to toe, Tucka Mertslin looked like a crow who'd been cheated out of an easy meal. Or was it a vulture?

Nurella waved to her fans, who were thanking their lucky stars that they had had the good sense to skip work that morning and the good fortune to see history being made. The sight of Nurella in the witness stand – alone, vulnerable and yet fiercely alive – had an eerie resemblance to her climactic confession scene in *Judgement at Limburg*. Even the details of her costume seemed familiar.

'We love you, Nurella!' someone squealed.

Nurella responded with a grateful smile.

In the fourth row of the balcony Corpius Crounce leaned forward, straining his eyes for a better look at her. It wasn't possible. And yet, it was her.

Nurella turned to Judge Maudlin. Her eyes, framed by their coal-black and impossibly long eyelashes, met his. Her whiskers trembled faintly. His twitched in response.

'I object!' bellowed Tucka. She slammed Nurella's framed photo on the table so hard that the glass shattered.

'But sweetie-pie,' said the judge, 'she hasn't said anything yet.'

'That's right,' Tucka seethed. 'And she shouldn't say a word until we see some identification!'

Judge Maudlin swallowed uncomfortably. 'That does seem reasonable, Miss Pinch. Would you happen to have any identification with you?'

'Well, Your Honour . . .' she began. She shifted uncomfortably in her chair and darted a nervous look at Hermux. 'I don't believe anyone has ever asked me for identification before.'

There were chuckles from her fans.

Tucka pounced immediately.

'Just as I thought,' she crowed with a poisonous smile. 'The witness is obviously an impostor. I move to strike her from the record.'

'Of course,' Nurella went on, 'I do have my driver's licence. If that would help.' She retrieved a wallet from her shoulder bag and opened it. 'I'm afraid it's not a very recent picture.' She handed her licence to the gopher, who handed it to the judge.

'Hmmm,' he said. He looked to Tucka and raised his eyebrows helplessly. 'It seems to be in order.'

'Your Honour!' Hermux implored. 'This is my witness, and I haven't even got to ask a question yet.'

'Oh, all right,' the judge said crankily. 'Ask some questions! But make it quick!'

Hermux put his hands in his pockets and rocked back on his heels in proper courtroom fashion.

'Are you really the one and only Nurella Pinch?' he asked her.

'Yes. I am.'

'And you are presently alive?'

Nurella held out her hands and examined them. 'To the best of my knowledge.'

'In the matter of your loan to Fluster Varmint –'

'Yes?'

Fluster sank uneasily into his chair. Beulith put her arm around him.

'Do you wish to foreclose on the theatre?'

'Of course not,' said Nurella. 'The theatre is his as long as he wishes to use it.' She looked directly at Beulith. 'And I bequeath it to his daughter after that.'

'Your Honour,' said Hermux, 'we rest our case!'

'Cross-examine!' Tucka insisted. An evil light flickered in her eyes as she approached the witness stand. 'Miss Pinch – if that is who you really are – is it not true that as the patient of Dr Hiril Mennus, you underwent certain beauty treatments that resulted in your total baldness?'

Nurella looked at her defiantly.

'Yes,' she said.

'Then if you really are the real Nurella Pinch, shouldn't you be bald?' Tucka jumped forward and grabbed Nurella's hat. She stepped back in triumph. She pointed at Nurella's neatly coiffed fur.

'See?' Tucka hopped victoriously from foot to foot. 'She's a phoney! I told you so! She's a phoney! The theatre is mine!'

Nurella rose slowly. For a brief moment she looked defeated. Then she drew herself up to a commanding height, looking down at Tucka with unmistakable pity.

'Is this what you meant?' she asked. Then very simply she reached up with both paws and lifted the wig from her bald head.

Tucka gasped. There was a moment of shocked silence in the courtroom. Then from the back a voice shouted, 'We love you, Nurella!' And the crowd leapt to its feet and joined in a whistling, stamping and standing ovation.

Chapter 57
PARTY ANIMALS

Fluster escorted Nurella out of the courtroom. There on the courthouse steps, surrounded by photographers and fans, they made an electrifying announcement. Nurella Pinch would return to the stage for a one-night-only special appearance at the gala premiere of Fluster Varmint's *Silver Jubilee Spectacular*. Then Nurella sped away in a limousine, and Varmint invited his jubilant crew back to the theatre to celebrate.

Beulith called ahead and ordered the kitchen opened. An hour later, the green room was jammed to capacity by the happy cast and crew and fans. Waiters rushed back and forth with trays of pizza, popcorn balls, cheese rolls, doughnuts, cake and ice cream. And the sound of popping corks filled the air.

'May I have your attention!' Fluster Varmint banged a bottle of Fizzy Bitters on the table to quiet the room. 'Ladies and gentlemen!' He extended his glass towards the Port-a-Pet and politely added, 'And esteemed bugs! I propose a toast!'

'A toast!' echoed the crowd.

'To happy endings!'

'To happy endings!'

'To Nurella Pinch!'

'To Nurella!'

'And to Hermux Tantamoq!' Varmint saluted Hermux. 'And a gentle reminder to Hermux that his design for the set is due first thing tomorrow morning! At the latest!'

Hermux nearly choked on his cake.

'Sputter! Gnawton! Chizzel!' commanded Varmint.

'Yes, sir!' they answered in unison.

'I want you on twenty-four-hour standby. We're opening our biggest show ever in two days! Did you hear that, Tantamoq? Two days! Now, enough with the celebration! We've got a show to do!' He drained his glass. 'And we're going to knock 'em dead! Now let's get to work!'

At Varmint's signal, the room began to clear. It was almost empty when Glissin arrived.

'Glissin!' exclaimed Beulith. 'I looked for you in court! You missed all the excitement! Nurella Pinch was absolutely sensational.'

'I heard,' she said, sounding very disappointed. 'I don't know what happened to me this morning. Of all mornings! I slept through my alarm and I just kept sleeping. It must be all the worrying.'

'Well, you can stop worrying!' said Beulith. She looked tenderly at her friend. 'Everything's OK now.'

'Still,' Glissin said dreamily, 'it would have been exciting to have seen her in person. It's been a long time.'

'Didn't you hear?' asked Beulith. 'She's coming back! And she asked for you specifically. She wants you to be her personal dresser. She won't work with anyone else.'

'Oh, my!' said Glissin. She was touched. 'How lovely! She actually remembers me?'

'More than that! She's your biggest fan,' said Beulith. 'Except for me, of course.'

Chapter 58
THE THRILL IS GONE

It was a slow afternoon at the Greasy Griddle. At the counter a waitress looked up from her paper.

'Who died?' she asked, eyeing Tucka's black dress and veil. She pointed to the booths. 'He's back there. Coffee? Or would you like a nice wooden stake?'

Tucka ignored her. She found Crounce. As she sat down, she decided to take a positive approach.

'Well?' she began. 'What do we do now?'

'We?' asked Crounce.

'We have to face facts, Corpius. As devious as it was, your plan didn't work.'

'*My* plan? That fiasco this morning wasn't my plan. My plan was to threaten Varmint. To put him in a vice and squeeze him until he cracked. And please take off that stupid veil! This isn't a funeral!'

Tucka lifted her veil. 'I was just trying to be discreet. Oh, Corpy!' she pleaded. 'Let's not quarrel. What difference does it make whose plan it was? I thought we were in this together.'

'Well,' thought Crounce as he listened. 'Why not? She's still a beautiful woman, and she's still rich.' He pictured the two of them together in a bank vault filled with gold. It was a very soothing image.

'My dearest! Of course we're in this together,' he said. 'Until death do us part.'

'Then we need to stay focused,' said Tucka. 'There must be another way to get that theatre. Think of something!'

But Crounce's thoughts were elsewhere. His interest in controlling the Varmint Theatre was waning fast. Running a theatre looked like a lot of dull work. Not nearly as easy as stealing. And not nearly as exciting. Besides, ever since he had seen Nurella Pinch in the courtroom, he had thought of very little else but her.

'Are you listening to me?' asked Tucka.

'Of course I'm listening,' said Crounce.

'Because if you're not interested, we don't have to go on with this.' She twisted the end of her veil into a hard knot. 'Of course, I have to wonder what Judge Maudlin would think if he knew that you had broken into Varmint's safe. And that your name is not really Corpius Crounce.'

Crounce responded with his most reassuring smile.

'Now, now,' he told her gently. 'There's no need to get nasty, darling. I'm thinking! That's all. I'm sure I'll come up with something.'

Chapter 59
GET READY! GET SET!

Hermux threw down his pencil in disgust.

'Who am I kidding?' he asked Terfle. 'I don't know how to design a set. I haven't had a single idea. Look at this!' He held up his sketchbook and thumbed the pages. 'Blank. Blank. Blank.'

Terfle pointed at the clock and marched in place.

'I know,' said Hermux. 'And it's leaving me behind.' He paced back and forth in front of his worktable. 'Everyone is counting on me. Even Nurella Pinch! And I can't let them down. I've got to come up with an idea!' He sat down again. 'Let's close our eyes and imagine opening night. The theatre is filled with people. The orchestra tunes up. Then the lights go down. It's pitch-dark. Everyone is waiting. Then – whoosh! – the curtain goes up! The stage lights come up. And there it is! Right there before their eyes! A great big –' Hermux opened his eyes and peeked at Terfle. 'Did you see anything?'

Terfle rubbed her eyes and shook her head.

'Me neither. We're in big trouble, aren't we?' said Hermux. He checked his watch. 'I don't suppose I have time to make a run to Lanayda's. I might think better if I had a little snack.'

Terfle gave the idea a thumbs down.

'You're right,' said Hermux. 'No more messing around.' He picked up his pencil with renewed determination and began to scribble wildly in his pad. Big loops at first. Followed by dense wiggles. Then a series of lightning bolts. Some wavy lines. And back-and-forth zigzags. When he had filled up the page, he stopped.

'Do you see anything?' he asked Terfle. They both squinted. 'This looks sort of like a cake, don't you think?'

Terfle wasn't sure.

'Speaking of cake,' said Hermux, 'I didn't even get to taste it at the party. Do you think there's any left? Let's go look! We could both use the exercise.' He tiptoed to the door and looked out into the hall. 'The coast is clear. Remember, we're supposed to be working, so if anyone sees us, we're just out getting a little air.'

Moving quickly and stealthily, Hermux walked down the hall to the green room and opened the door without making a sound. He slipped inside and closed the door as quietly as he had opened it. He surveyed the remains of the party.

'Look at that! There's a whole trayful of popcorn balls. Hardly touched! And that cake must be here somewhere.' Hermux opened the Port-a-Pet. 'Scout around and see what you can find.'

Terfle immediately took to the air.

'Mmmmm! Pretzel rods!' said Hermux, finding a bowlful on the floor next to the couch. He popped one into his mouth. 'You have to take the salty with the sweet!' Hermux's mood was getting brighter by the moment. 'First, we'll have a great big satisfying snack! And then we're going to design the most beautiful set of all time!'

Terfle buzzed by excitedly and signalled Hermux to follow.

She led him to the back of the room. There on a table behind an armchair sat the enormous cake. It was a five-layer lemon cake with turquoise frosting and raspberry jam between the layers. Only one piece was missing.

'Oh, my!' said Hermux. His heart pounded. 'That is beautiful! And look how much there is!' On an impulse he began to stick the pretzels one by one into the frosting. 'Happy birthday to us!' he sang softly. 'Happy birthday to us!'

Next Terfle found a whole jar of maraschino cherries, and Hermux poured it over the cake. The luscious cherries plopped into the turquoise frosting, and the ruby syrup pooled across the top and dripped down the sides.

'It looks delicious!' said Hermux. He placed the cake carefully on the platter that had held the popcorn balls, and he decorated the sides of the cake with the balls. 'There! That should hold us, even if we have to work all night.' He motioned Terfle back into her cage. 'Now let's get out of here!' He balanced the hefty snack tray on one hand and reached for the Port-a-Pet with the other. Then he stopped suddenly. 'Wait a minute!' he said. 'What's that?'

It was a doughnut. Sitting all by itself on a saucer. Chocolate-coconut. With candy sprinkles. Hermux lifted it tenderly and took a small bite.

'Perfect!' he said. He was about to take another bite when there were sounds of heavy footsteps outside the door. Someone was coming!

Hermux looked for a place to hide. There was no closet. The biggest thing in the room was the couch, which sat against a wall. He jammed the doughnut on top of the cake, grabbed the Port-a-Pet, and made for the couch. He hooked one foot behind it and yanked it forward, creating just enough space for him, the

215

cake and the Port-a-Pet. He pushed them both inside and crawled in behind as the door opened and someone came in. Hermux watched beneath the couch as a pair of large feet crossed the room towards the back.

A deep voice hummed contentedly and then stopped abruptly.

'Where is it?' the voice demanded. 'I hid it right here!'

Hermux held his breath. He recognized the voice. It was Varmint. He was looking for the cake. Hermux eyed it guiltily. Gazing up from where he lay, the cake appeared even more beautiful than he remembered. Crowned with its standing doughnut and ringed by rows of salted pretzels, cherries and popcorn balls, it towered like a monument to all the great desserts of history. It was so magnificent that it made his mouth water just to look at it.

There were sounds of furniture being dragged and shoved.

'Somebody stole my cake!' Varmint said irritably. 'I can't believe it! You can't trust anyone any more!'

'What should we do?' Hermux whispered. Terfle pointed at the cake. She clapped. She took a bow. Hermux looked again. Terfle was right about the cake, and she didn't even like sweets. Cakes like that didn't come along every day. It deserved a big round of applause. 'In fact,' he thought, 'this cake belongs onstage.'

'Terfle!' he said out loud. 'You're a genius!'

Terfle took another bow.

'Who's there?' demanded Varmint. 'Who is it?'

Hermux got to his feet.

'It's me,' he said. 'And Terfle.' He hoisted up the Port-a-Pet and set it on the couch.

'What are you doing hiding behind the couch?' Varmint asked.

'We wanted to surprise you,' said Hermux.

'What kind of surprise?'

'We have something to show you.' Hermux lifted the cake into view. 'It's for the *Jubilee*. Happy silver anniversary!'

As Fluster approached the couch, his eyes twitched from the cake to Hermux to Terfle. And back to the cake. He opened his mouth to speak. But nothing came out.

'What do you think?' Hermux asked nervously.

Fluster pointed at the cake. He shook his head violently, rattling his jowls. Then he put two fingers in his mouth and gave an ear-punishing whistle. It was answered by shouts from the hallway. In moments Sputter, Gnawton and Chizzel burst into the room.

'Right here, boss! What's up?'

Varmint pointed accusingly at Hermux.

Hermux prepared himself to be thrown out of the theatre. He came out from behind the couch and surrendered the cake to Varmint.

Varmint held it up high for Sputter, Gnawton and Chizzel to see. 'Take a good look, boys!' he thundered. 'I think we've got ourselves a set!'

Hermux was too relieved to respond properly. But it didn't matter. Varmint wasn't listening anyway. He was already on his way to the set shop, barking orders at Sputter, Gnawton and Chizzel, who followed fast behind. As he bustled through the door he shouted back over his shoulder, 'I knew you could do it, Tantamoq! And I'm never wrong!'

Hermux and Terfle found themselves alone again.

'I think we did it,' said Hermux. 'Thanks to you, Terfle! We designed the set! I can't believe it. Let's go tell Glissin!' He lifted the Port-a-Pet up on to his shoulder and started towards the costume shop. He marched triumphantly out of the green room and ran right into the flying squirrel.

'Glory be!' said the flying squirrel. 'Tantamoq at last! I've been looking for you all over town!' He handed Hermux a telegram.

Hermux set down the Port-a-Pet and ripped open the envelope.

ARRIVE PINCHESTER LATE AFTERNOON
STOP   CELEBRATION AT ROOTS SIX PM
STOP BIG ANNOUNCEMENT   STOP   HOPE YOU
CAN BE THERE   STOP   LINKA

'It's almost six o'clock now!' groaned Hermux. 'Why didn't you get this to me earlier?'

'What can I say?' said the squirrel. 'It's been a busy day. Girl trouble?'

'How did you know?'

'Your paws are shaking.'

Hermux put them behind his back.

'Listen, buddy, if you need any advice, I'm an expert on the female mind. From A to Z. And none of that college stuff either. I'm talking personal experience. And my rates are very competitive.'

Chapter 60
FOOLS RUSH IN

Terfle gripped the bars of her cage and leaned into the wind as Hermux zigged and zagged through the busy streets of Pinchester.

'We must be getting close,' he panted.

The scent of roasting vegetables was unmistakable. Hermux quickened his pace and followed his nose. The tantalizing aromas of onions, carrots and potatoes drifted down the street. There was rosemary too, and butter. And maybe a hint of pepper. Hermux's stomach growled. But hunger was not what was driving Hermux. He wanted to see Linka. But what was she celebrating? And what was she going to announce?

At the next corner hung a red neon sign.

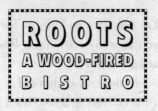

'That must be it,' said Hermux. 'Keep your fingers crossed!'

Terfle didn't have fingers. She crossed her antennae instead.

Heart pounding, Hermux squared his shoulders and opened the door. Roots was warm, dark and noisy inside. It was not very big, and most of the space was taken up by the open kitchen, which stood in the middle of the room. A high counter surrounded the kitchen. In its centre was a brick oven mounded with glowing coals. A blur of chefs in tall white hats bustled about, magically avoiding collisions as they chopped vegetables, dipped them in butter, and shovelled them into and out of the coals. People ate standing at the counter or seated at tiny tables pushed up against the walls.

Someone waved at him from the counter. It was Linka. She stood with her arm draped casually over someone's shoulder. He wore an earring in his ear.

After a day of triumphs, it was hard for Hermux to believe that his luck had finally run out. But apparently it had. He hoisted the Port-a-Pet on to his shoulder and turned to leave. He wasn't ready to face Brinx and Linka as a couple.

'Hermux! Come back!' Linka shouted.

Hermux paused. He was trapped.

Brinx cupped his hands and shouted, 'Could everyone pipe down for a moment? I've got an important announcement to make.' Then he climbed up on a stool and stepped on to the bar. He turned to face the crowd. To Hermux's amazement, it wasn't Brinx at all.

'Hi!' he said. 'I'm Buzzer Von Tointin, for those of you who don't know me. And this is my restaurant, Roots. Tonight we're celebrating our first anniversary!'

'Hurray for Roots!' the crowd shouted.

'Thank you!' Buzzer took a bow. 'We'll get right back to celebrating, but first I've got an announcement to make. At Roots we try to make every meal an adventure in dining. And to

220

demonstrate our commitment to adventure, I'm announcing tonight that we will be sponsoring Pinchester's premier adventuress in next month's coast-to-coast fly-off. Racing for Roots will be none other than my old friend Linka Perflinger!'

Hermux didn't know whether to laugh or cry.

'Speech!' the crowd demanded.

Linka climbed up on the bar.

'Thank you, Buzzer!' she said. 'It's a tremendous honour to be here tonight. And an honour to be racing for Roots. And I will be racing to win! But there's something very important I want to say. Not too long ago I had given up adventure and flying. I even put my plane up for sale. I nearly gave up on my dreams. And if it weren't for one mouse who believed in me, those dreams would have died. If it weren't for him, I wouldn't be here tonight. And I want to thank him. Ladies and gentlemen, join me in a round of applause for Mr Hermux Tantamoq!' She blew Hermux a kiss.

'Drinks are on the house!' said Buzzer.

'Hooray for Linka. Hooray for Hermux!' yelled the crowd.

'Hooray for everyone,' yelled Hermux. Terfle seconded that with her bell.

When the hubbub had died down, Buzzer found them a table in the corner.

'I'm honoured to meet you,' Buzzer told Hermux. He brought a high chair for the Port-a-Pet. 'No menus for you tonight. I'll take care of everything. And I'll find something for you too,' he told Terfle.

Linka leaned forward on the table. 'Well, what do you think?'

'I think you're the most beautiful mouse in the world.'

Linka smiled, then smoothed her whiskers self-consciously. 'No, silly. I mean the announcement. I'm going to be racing again.'

'I think that's beautiful too. I think the whole world is beautiful!'

The waiter delivered a platter of crispy onion rings.

'Compliments of the house,' he said.

The smell was delicious. But for Hermux it was not nearly as delicious as the sight of Linka's dear face. She was home again from the skies. Safe and sound. And surprising as always. Hermux grew very serious.

'But what about your screen test?'

'I'd rather not talk about it while we're eating,' she said. She popped an onion ring into her mouth.

'Oh,' said Hermux.

'I don't want to get sick.'

'That bad?'

'Two words.'

'What?'

'Slimy lips. There! I said it.' She ate another onion ring. 'I guess I'm starting to recover. Please, let's not talk about Brinx. I've had enough. Tell me what you've been doing.'

'I've been thinking a lot,' he said.

'About the theatre?'

'Yes. I mean no. I've been thinking about you. About us. You and me.'

'How sweet! What have you been thinking?'

'It's now or never,' thought Hermux. He glanced at the Port-a-Pet. Terfle had climbed up on to her perch. She nodded encouragingly.

'Linka, there's something I need to tell you – I mean – I've

222

come to realize that – the thing is – a time comes in a mouse's life when – I – ' He looked desperately into Linka's eyes. 'I love you!'

At 9:00 a.m. the next morning, tickets for the gala opening starring Nurella Pinch went on sale. The line outside the Varmint Theatre extended around the block. By 11:15 the show was sold out. At 11:16 Varmint declared that the era of dinner theatre was officially over. He called a moving company to remove the dining tables and chairs from the auditorium. The theatre seats came out of storage and were reinstalled in rows. Seating capacity doubled. At noon the box office reopened. By 1:00 the additional tickets were gone.

The *Silver Jubilee Spectacular* would be the biggest hit of Fluster Varmint's career. Beulith had never been so proud of her father. Varmint had never been so relieved in his life.

Rehearsals started at two. Downstairs, Sputter, Gnawton and Chizzel hammered and sawed. They plastered. They painted. They yodelled as they worked. Layer by layer a giant cake began to rise. Across the hall Glissin cut and sewed as Terfle watched with a critical eye. Next door Hermux happily packed his tools.

It would be sad to leave the theatre. There was no doubt about it. Hermux loved his new friends, and he had enjoyed all the excitement. Or at least most of it. But he wouldn't be sorry to get back to his cosy, quiet shop and get on with his own life. It seemed like things were getting back on track. He had helped to save the theatre. He and Terfle had managed to design the set. And best of all, he and Linka were in love.

'I've never been so happy,' thought Hermux. 'It's wonderful just to be alive.' Then he remembered Termind the parrot, who was no longer alive. And he realized that his work at the theatre was not quite over.

Chapter 62
SQUEEZE PLAY

'What's so hard to remember?' asked Magner Wooliun. 'Your thumb turns the head. Your index finger controls the beak. Your middle finger flaps the wings. And your pinky lifts the tail. Now try it again from the top. And pay attention.'

'I can't do it!' said Binter. 'It's too complicated. Besides, it gives me the creeps. You should have thought about that before.'

Magner ignored him. 'Just one more time,' he coaxed. 'Practice makes perfect. Now put on the glove!'

Reluctantly Binter slipped his hand into the glove. He wiggled his fingers and the parrot's body jerked to life. 'I hate this!' he said.

He raised the parrot and held it out at shoulder height. He turned the parrot's head to face him. Then he bared his teeth in a grimace and, raising his voice an octave, he began. 'So, tell me!' he squawked. 'What's a nice shrew like you doing in a dump like this?'

'When the parrot talks, move the parrot's mouth, not yours!' Magner was running out of patience.

'It's not my fault!' complained Binter. 'I was doing just fine until you came along. Mr Big Shot with his big plans! And his

226

big pay-off! "Just get me inside the theatre," you said. "I'll take care of everything," you said. "A one-way ticket to Easy Street!" Well, you took care of it, all right! And now I got a one-way ticket to nowhere!'

'Little Binter!' taunted Magner. 'You never see the big picture, do you?'

'I can see that I'm getting the shaft! And I'm through covering for you!'

Magner moved with lightning speed. He grabbed the shrew's tail and yanked his feet out from under him. Binter hit the floor face down. Magner leapt on his back and clamped his throat in a hammerlock.

'I had to shut the parrot's mouth,' he hissed. 'And I can shut yours too.' He increased the pressure on Binter's windpipe.

'I can't breathe!' gasped Binter.

'Funny! That's exactly what the parrot said.' He released Binter as suddenly as he had pinned him.

Binter sat up, wheezing. He rubbed his neck. 'You didn't have to do that!'

'Yes, I did,' said Magner coldly. 'Besides, I enjoyed it. Now get up. I've got another assignment for you. I want you to find out when Nurella Pinch is coming to the theatre and which dressing room she's using.'

A sly smile crossed Binter's face.

'What?' said Magner.

'So Mr Know-it-all doesn't know everything!'

'What does that mean?'

'It means that I may not be much of a ventriloquist, but I've got an ear for voices. I heard her in the courtroom. If it's Nurella Pinch you want, talk to Glissin. She's your girl!'

Chapter 63
THREAD BARE

The apprentice slipped through the curtains and left the stage, making no more sound than a snake passing through summer grass. Then he glided downstairs in search of his prey. When he arrived at the costume shop, the door was wide open. He stood for a moment and watched the scene inside with considerable interest.

Beulith stood before the mirror in a party dress. Its pale blue chiffon was a perfect compliment to her beige fur. Beside her knelt Glissin, pinning the hem.

'We're nearly finished,' she managed to say through a mouthful of pins.

Binter had obviously made a mistake. This could not be Nurella Pinch. Even in a disguise. Glissin was pathetic. Cheerful and dutiful, the way pathetic people tended to be. There was no trace of regal bearing. No trace of emotional fire. This was not the first woman he had ever loved – or at least pretended to love. If this was Nurella Pinch in disguise, then he was Fluster Varmint's uncle!

At that moment he caught sight of someone in the mirror. The man wore a shapeless suit in a bilious green. He had wiry hair growing from his ears. And eyeglasses held together with tape. A horrified expression crept over the man's face. No wonder. It was him! He did look like Varmint's uncle.

As he continued to watch her work, he realized that the woman before him was no ordinary costume mistress. Everything about her was perfect to the smallest detail. The way she held the pins in her mouth. The way she lovingly stretched and draped the fabric before she pinned it. The way she nodded attentively as she listened to Beulith make small talk about her new boyfriend, who worked in a watch shop, and their big date for the gala performance. Every one of Glissin's gestures was exactly right. Unstudied. Effortless. Spontaneous. It was glaringly obvious. The whole thing was an act. An award-worthy performance.

Glissin got to her feet and stood behind Beulith, admiring the young mouse's reflection in the mirror. She smoothed the fur on Beulith's bare shoulder.

'I think Nip is a very lucky young man,' she said.

'I think he is too,' said Beulith with a laugh. 'Oh, Glissin! It's a beautiful dress! I can't believe you took time to make it in the middle of all this chaos. Thank you! I wish Mother were here to see it!'

'She is,' said Glissin tenderly. 'She's watching over you right now. And she's smiling.'

Beulith turned. 'You really think so?'

Glissin nodded and smiled.

'I don't know how I would have grown up without you!' declared Beulith. She threw her arms around Glissin and hugged her affectionately.

'Now I get it!' the appentice thought. 'She's too old to be a star herself any longer. So she's grooming the girl to take her

229

place as the next Nurella Pinch. She's created her own Frankenstar! Someone who will do her bidding! Someone she can control! Wouldn't it be too bad if I spoiled her plans! What if something awful were to happen to the lovely young Beulith? But it will be more than just a close call this time. Poor Varmint! Poor Nurella! Why, it would be like killing two birds with one stone.'

'Now, you get changed so I can get this finished,' Glissin told Beulith. As Beulith disappeared into the dressing room, Glissin noticed him standing there.

'You're the ventriloquist's apprentice, aren't you?' asked Glissin, setting her pins aside. 'I hope you're not here for a costume. It's a little late for that.'

'Oh, no,' said the apprentice, acting awkward and embarrassed. 'No costume for me yet. I'm still just learning. It's Mr Binter. He wanted me to tell you that his jacket fits perfectly. And to say thank you.'

'Why, that's very nice of him,' said Beulith. 'You tell him that he's welcome.'

Beulith emerged from the dressing room, carrying her party dress on a hanger. 'I've got to get back to work too. I don't know how we're going to be ready by tomorrow night.'

'We always manage,' said Glissin.

'Yes, we do, don't we?' Beulith kissed Glissin on the cheek before she hurried away.

Moments after she had gone, the apprentice reappeared in the doorway.

'Such a lovely young girl,' he said.

There was something suggestive in his tone that Glissin didn't care for.

'Yes, she is,' she replied cautiously.

'Could I have a word with you?' To Glissin's astonishment, he closed the shop door and locked it. 'It might be better if we spoke in private.' The ventriloquist's apprentice seemed to have lost all traces of shyness.

'Who are you?' Glissin demanded.

'Don't tell me that you've forgotten me,' said the apprentice. 'We had such good times together!' He pulled the hair plugs from his ears. He raked his claws through his fur and smiled. It was a perfect smile. 'It's been too long, my fuzzy little peach. Much too long.'

Glissin's heart froze. Only one person in the world had ever called her his 'fuzzy little peach'. Only one person had that perfect smile – and used it as a weapon. His name was Purvit Klimpsheeler, her dancing partner in the original Okey-Dokey Girls. The first man she had ever loved. The first man who had betrayed her, broken her heart and deserted her. She felt as though a bandage had been ripped off an old wound. And it was not healed.

'Purvit?' she gasped. 'No! It can't be you. Not after all this time! Not now!'

'There's no time like the present, baby!' he said. 'Have you missed me? How about a kiss?' He reached for her, and she recoiled. 'Not even for old times' sake?'

'You mean the old times of using me, lying to me, cheating on me and then leaving me without even saying goodbye?' The dutiful, helpful Glissin was gone. It was Nurella Pinch who spoke, and she was angry. 'What do you want?'

'That's a bit one-sided, don't you think?'

'And did I forget to mention the little detail of your stealing on the side? Picking pockets in the audience? Pilfering hotel rooms? You put all of us at risk so you could wear silk suits and handmade shoes.'

'I put you at risk? You should talk!' Crounce shot back. He circled around her slowly. 'You don't think I know who ratted me out? You and your little friend Beulene! Couldn't keep your mouth shut, could you? And I was the one with talent! Not you! I was the one who was destined for stardom. You were nobody! Nobody!'

'And who are you now, Purvit?'

'Forget Purvit! He's gone. You killed him. You crushed him and his dreams, you and Varmint and the rest of you hypocrites! And now you're all going to pay! Look at you! The great Nurella Pinch. What a joke! People say you lost your mind, you know. What would they say if they saw you like this?'

'They won't.'

'What if I tell them?'

'Why would you?'

'To teach you a lesson.'

'You taught me plenty of lessons. I haven't forgotten any of them.'

'There's always more to learn. Humility, for example.'

'Learn humility from you?' Nurella laughed bitterly. 'That's rich.' She began to unlock the door. 'You walked out on me once. This time I'm throwing you out!'

He pushed her from the door and blocked it with his body.

'I'm not through yet.' He sneered. 'I know what you're up to! And I intend to put a stop to it!'

'You don't know anything about me!'

'You don't fool me. I know that you're grooming little Beulith to be a star – to be the next Nurella Pinch! You've been holed up here like a spider spinning a web around her. Creating your little puppet to be the star you'll never be again!'

'That's what you really think?' she asked.

He responded with a smile of ice. 'Hit a nerve, didn't I?'

'You've hit rock bottom! The great actor, my handsome Prince Charming . . . you think I'm pathetic? Look at yourself! You're nothing, a cheap crook. But that's what you were all along, isn't it? You think you can still hurt me? You're wrong. But you leave Beulith out of this, or so help me, I'll –'

'You'll what? Report me to your little watchmaker friend?

Don't make me laugh! And as for Beulith – I was thinking: It would be a pity if something were to happen to that pretty face of hers. Or if she were unable to walk.' He paused for effect. 'Or breathe.'

'You would do that?'

'I would do more, if that is what it takes to cut you down to size.'

'Just to get back at me,' she asked, 'you would hurt your own daughter?'

Chapter 65
FAMILY VALUES

'My daughter?' he said as though he had been kicked in the stomach.

'*Our* daughter,' said Nurella.

His mind raced to calculate the possibilities that she was telling the truth. The calculations ended with an image of Beulith lying unconscious on the stage, surrounded by the debris of the shattered spotlight. The floor under his feet buckled and swayed. He staggered to a chair and collapsed as waves of nausea swept over him. Nurella had cheated him of the joys of fatherhood. The rights. The privileges. The pride!

'You waited until now to tell me?'

'It's the first time I've seen you.'

'You could have made an effort!'

'You left me. Remember?'

'You could have tracked me down!'

'How?' she asked. 'And why? You were done with me. I think that was your word. *Done*. And why would I want my child to have a thief for a father?'

'But she was my child!' He was indignant. 'I had a right to know!'

'You lost it.'

'Well, now I've regained it. And the question is, what am I going to do with it?'

Nurella brandished a pair of scissors in her hands. 'I wouldn't hesitate to kill you,' she said. She took a step towards him.

'Ah, the noble Nurella! At last!' He snickered and waved away the scissors. 'Don't kid yourself, kiddo. This isn't the movies! You wouldn't know where to begin.' He put on his glasses. 'How much does she know, anyway?'

'She doesn't know anything. I gave her to Varmint and Beulene when she was born. They raised her. Until Beulene passed away. And then I came.'

'Mommy dearest!' he sniped. He fitted the plugs of hair back into his ears and got up to leave.

'Where are you going?'

'You're throwing me out. Remember? I'm going for a walk. To think things over.'

Nurella grabbed his arm in desperation. 'What are you going to do?'

'I'll let you know tomorrow night. After your gala performance! I'll make it a surprise.'

'Leave us alone,' Nurella begged. 'Just leave us alone!'

His perfect smile returned.

'Break a leg!' he told her.

It was nearly closing time, and except for the shuffling of cards and the ticking of twenty-seven clocks, Hermux's shop was dead quiet. Nip stopped and placed the deck of playing cards face down on the counter.

'You're sure you remember your card?' Hermux asked.

'Yep!'

'All right, then, cut them.'

Nip split the deck in half and restacked it.

'Now fan them out.'

Nip spread the cards across the surface of the counter. 'Like this?' he asked.

'That's it,' Hermux told him. 'Terfle, your blindfold.'

Terfle fastened an extremely small black scarf across her eyes. Then Hermux set her down at one end of the cards. She walked along the edge of the deck. Then she stopped and tapped the corner of a card with one foot.

Hermux removed the card from the deck and held it up. 'The jack of diamonds,' he said.

'That's it!' exclaimed Nip.

Terfle took a bow.

'How does she do it?'

'She's not telling,' said Hermux. 'Just don't bet her any money. I learned that the hard way.'

'I want her to hypnotize me!' said Nip. 'Like she did the cricket.'

'I don't know,' said Hermux. 'What if you don't come out of it?'

Terfle ran to the Port-a-Pet to retrieve her sequin, and was just rolling it across the counter when the door opened and the flying squirrel strolled in. He spotted the cards immediately and headed straight for them.

'Private game? Or can anyone play? I feel lucky today.'

'Sorry,' said Hermux. 'You just missed the last hand. What have you got for me?'

The squirrel withdrew a large brown envelope. It was from the Varmint Theatre, but it was not Varmint's handwriting. Hermux opened it.

'It's from Beulith,' he said. 'It's the programme for the gala tonight.'

Taped to its cover was a note.

> Dear Hermux and Terfle,
>
> Hot off the press! I thought you would like to see this.
>
> Beulith
>
> P.S. Look at page 4.

Eagerly Hermux opened the programme. 'Listen to this! "Scenery designed by Hermux Tantamoq and Terfle."' He held

the page out for Terfle to see. 'We can put it in our scrapbook.'
Then he showed it to Nip. And finally to the squirrel. 'That's us!'
he bragged.

'So, now that you're rich, I suppose you'll be closing the
shop,' observed the squirrel.

'Rich?' asked Hermux. 'When did I get rich?'

'I thought all theatre people were rich.'

'What gave you that idea?'

'That's a pretty fancy boat that fellow's got. And he's a theatre
person.'

'What fellow?'

'Magner Wooliun. And he's just a ventriloquist's apprentice.
I figure they must be paying you plenty more than him.'

'Magner Wooliun, huh?' Hermux was intrigued. 'What kind
of boat does he have? Where is it? And how do you know?'

'Ah! We're curious, are we?' said the squirrel. His tail
rippled with anticipation, and his black eyes sparkled with greed.
'That kind of information doesn't come cheap.'

'I didn't think it would,' grumbled Hermux. 'How much?'

'Ten dollars.'

'All right,' Hermux agreed. 'What do you know?'

'Just this. An hour ago, we get a call from the marina. I
make the pickup. And it's this Magner guy. From the Varmint.
He lives on a boat. A very pricey boat!'

'What did you pick up?' Hermux wanted to know.

'Tantamoq!' the squirrel scolded. 'I'm shocked at you. Our
work is strictly confidential!'

'How much?' asked Hermux.

'Fifteen.'

'Put it on my tab!'

'He gave me this.' The squirrel showed Hermux an envelope.

239

It was addressed to Tucka Mertslin. 'I'm on my way over there now.'

Hermux grabbed for the envelope, but the squirrel held it out of reach.

'Naughty! Naughty! Mustn't read other people's mail!'

'I need to see that!' said Hermux.

'Twenty dollars.'

'That's outrageous!'

'You're asking me to break a solemn oath,' said the squirrel.

'OK,' Hermux conceded. 'Give it to me. I can steam it open, and she'll never know.'

'No need,' said the squirrel. 'I can tell you what it says.'

'You already read it?' It was Hermux's turn to be shocked.

'Of course I did. It pays to stay informed.' He cracked a sunflower seed and spit the shell on the floor. Then he began to recite.

My dearest and most devious darling,

Good news at last! I've got something that should cause quite an explosion at the theatre. Meet me there tonight and we'll pick up the pieces!

Love and kisses,
Corpius Crounce

'So Magner isn't his real name at all!' Hermux whispered to Nip. 'And I was right about his not being a real apprentice. He's working undercover like me. But he's working for Tucka. And now he's discovered a new secret to blackmail Varmint with!'

'What kind of secret?' asked Nip.

'Who knows? said Hermux. 'They're theatre people. Varmint has probably got hundreds of secrets.' Hermux turned back to the squirrel. 'Is there anything else?' he asked.

'There's a ticket for the show tonight. A good seat too. Say, I wouldn't mind going if you could get me a seat.'

'Sorry,' said Hermux. 'They're sold out.'

'Typical,' said the squirrel. He stowed Crounce's letter in his pouch, then extended a familiar paw. 'That will be sixty dollars. Five for regular delivery, and fifty-five for custom services.'

Hermux took the deck of cards from the counter and began to shuffle them.

'So, you like cards?' he asked, giving the squirrel a playful wink. 'My friend Terfle here is just learning how to play.'

Chapter 67
AIRBORNE

Chapter 67
AIRBORNE

When the squirrel left the shop, he was poorer, but wiser. Hermux immediately called the theatre. Varmint could not come to the phone.

'I've got to talk to him,' Hermux urged Oaf. 'Tell him it's an emergency!'

'Everything's an emergency!' replied the harried hedgehog. 'It's a madhouse here. If you want to talk to him, get over here and stand in line with the rest of us!'

Hermux and Terfle rushed home, changed into their evening attire, and set off immediately for the Varmint. Linka would meet them at the theatre before the performance. In the meantime, he and Terfle would find out what they could about Crounce and his explosive secret.

'Look!' cried Hermux as they approached Bracken Street. Overhead, two brilliant beams of light crisscrossed the darkening sky. 'It really is a gala premiere!' He held the Port-a-Pet up so Terfle could see the spotlights. 'Do you suppose anyone will want our autographs?'

Terfle didn't answer. Something strange was happening in the street behind them. A dark and sinister shape hovered in the air. It was moving straight towards them and gaining speed.

Terfle waved to Hermux. But he was preoccupied with Crounce and Tucka. She pointed and hopped up and down. Hermux was oblivious. She ran to the emergency bell and yanked its cord with all her strength. An ominous creaking filled the air.

Hermux turned. But it was too late! It was already upon them. A grotesque flying creature with outstretched claws. So huge, it blocked out the sky as it passed overhead. Hermux knew immediately – this was Crounce's surprise for Tucka! He had somehow brought this monster to Pinchester and intended to hold the theatre for ransom! But how was he controlling it?

Looking closer, Hermux could see that the monster was restrained by heavy ropes leashed to a tractor-trailer truck. One look at the cab of the truck confirmed his suspicions. At the wheel, illuminated by the glow of the instrument panel, sat Tucka herself. For a brief instant their eyes met. Then Tucka reached for the dashboard and flipped a switch. She was setting the creature loose on him and Terfle!

Hermux threw the Port-a-Pet to the ground and covered it with his body.

'You'll have to kill me first!' he cried defiantly. As he prepared himself to be torn to bits, he tried to turn his last thoughts towards Linka. But before he could focus his mind, the truck moved on, pulling its cargo behind it. Hermux scrambled to his feet just as the theatre's roving spotlights came together and focused on the creature.

Hermux screamed.

It was an inflatable, flying Tucka in a hot-pink bodysuit with a purple cape that billowed behind her. The trailer below was ablaze with neon.

Chapter 68
STAGE FRIGHT

Varmint moved through the theatre like a general barking last-minute orders to his troops before a battle. Behind him ran Beulith and Oaf, shouting questions and taking notes. And behind all of them ran Hermux. With Terfle along for the ride.

Hermux tried and tried again to get Varmint's attention.

'Not now!' he said. 'No time!'

They raced across the auditorium, up the stairs to the stage, around the stage to the dressing rooms, down the stairs to the basement, and back up the stairs to the lobby. And then they started over. By their second lap Hermux was panting hard. When he spotted a dressing room marked NURELLA PINCH, he gave up the chase.

'I need water,' he told Terfle. 'Besides, we need to talk to Glissin. Maybe she knows what Crounce is up to.'

The sign on the door was very explicit.

> *Please respect*
> *Miss Pinch's privacy.*
> **NO VISITORS!**

Hermux knocked anyway. Glissin answered the door in her usual apron. She looked tired.

'Shouldn't you be . . . getting ready?' enquired Hermux.

She closed the door behind them and locked it. She sat down at the dressing table and examined her face in the mirror. She opened a jar of make-up. Then without warning she hurled it against the wall.

'Look at me!' she screamed. 'I can't do it! I can't go out there in front of a sold-out house and act and sing and dance like nothing's happened! I'm not a miracle worker!' She collapsed in sobs.

'But I thought the show had to go on,' said Hermux. 'And all that.'

'The show?' asked Glissin. 'This time, it's going to have to go on without me.'

'It can't,' said Hermux. 'You *are* the show. Everyone is counting on you. You can't let them down now.'

'I've already let them down,' said Glissin. 'Everyone that matters. I've made a horrible mess of things!'

'No,' said Hermux. 'You saved the theatre!'

'I thought I had. But there was only one reason to save it. And now it's gone. And it's all because of me.'

'You're not making sense,' said Hermux.

'Sadly, it's probably the first time in my life that I *am* making sense.'

'I'm slow. You have to explain.'

'Why not?' she conceded. 'It's all over, anyway!'

Neither Hermux nor Terfle said a word.

'I'm sorry,' she said. 'I forgot how melodramatic Nurella is! I'll try to keep it simple. When I was very young, I fell in love with someone, and I thought he loved me. But he

246

didn't. That sounds like the beginning of a bad movie, doesn't it? He left me. And after he left, I found out I was pregnant. I had a daughter. I couldn't raise her, so I gave her to my best friend. Then my best friend died. And my daughter needed a mother.'

The story was beginning to sound familiar to Hermux.

'Beulith?' said Hermux.

Glissin nodded. 'I never saw her father again. Until yesterday. He tracked me down. He's been working here. Now he says he wants to punish me.'

'For what?' asked Hermux.

'He thought he was going to be a star. But what he really was was a thief. He got caught and Varmint kicked him out of the theatre. He thinks I turned him in. Now he blames me and Varmint for ruining his life. But that doesn't matter. What matters is that now he knows about our daughter.'

'About Beulith?'

'Yes. Beulith. Like the fool I've always been, I told him about her. I was trying to protect her. But what I did was put her at risk.'

Hermux remembered the smiling mouse who stood behind Nurella on the poster of the Okey-Dokey Girls – the handsome mouse who had seemed so familiar. It was Magner Wooliun – alias Corpius Crounce.

'It's the ventriloquist's apprentice, isn't it?' he asked.

Glissin nodded.

'But what can he do to her?' asked Hermux.

'For starters, he can tell Beulith that her whole life has been a lie. That her real father is a thief.'

Hermux thought it over. 'And her real mother is Nurella Pinch. Is that so bad?'

'I'm not sure it's anything to be proud of,' said Glissin.

'Then I think you'd better go out there and put on a show that'll make her proud to be your daughter!'

Chapter 69
BEHIND CLOSED DOORS

Chapter 69
BEHIND CLOSED DOORS

Moments after they left, there was another knock at the door. Glissin opened it, expecting to see Hermux again.

'What did you forget?' she asked.

But it wasn't Hermux. It was Brinx Lotelle. He was toting a movie camera.

'Hi, doll,' he said, trying to look around her into the dressing room. 'These are for Nurella.' He thrust a handful of daisies at her. 'Tell her they're from Brinx.'

'I'll tell Miss Pinch that you called,' said Glissin. She began to shut the door. Brinx jammed his foot in the way.

'Maybe you didn't hear me,' he said. 'Tell her Brinx is here. Brinx Lotelle? Maybe the name rings a bell? The action film director? She'll want to see me. I'm making a movie about her.' When Glissin didn't respond, he attempted to push her out of the way. But Glissin was not to be moved.

'She's not here yet,' she said, blocking the door firmly. She looked faintly amused.

'No way!' Brinx argued. 'The show starts in twenty minutes.'

Glissin stepped back and held the door wide open.

'See for yourself.'

Except for a rack of costumes, the dressing room was empty.

'Don't worry,' Glissin reassured him. 'She is famous for arriving late. But she's never missed a curtain.'

Glissin looked around to see if there was anyone who might overhear her.

'Look, you seem like a nice guy, so I'll let you in on a secret,' she whispered. 'But for goodness' sake, don't tell anyone I told you. The fans have been driving her crazy. So she moved. This isn't her real dressing room. It's just a decoy. The real one is downstairs. It's not even marked. I can take you down there. But we have to move fast. You can't be seen or I'll lose my job!'

'Lead the way,' he said.

With Brinx right behind her, Glissin scurried down the stairs, past the set shop, and turned into Hermux's old workroom. At the back was a door marked STORAGE. She removed a ring of keys from an apron pocket, chose one, unlocked the door, and opened it.

'Quick!' she said. 'She's in here!' Brinx rushed inside. Glissin slammed the door behind him and locked it. Then she switched off the lights and hurried back to her dressing room to get changed.

'It might turn out to be a nice evening after all,' she thought.

Chapter 70
CURTAINS

At five minutes to eight, the box office received an emergency telephone call. The train from Twyrp had just arrived one hour late. On it were 117 members of the Twyrp chapter of the Nurella Pinch Fan Club. Speaking for the hysterical members of his club, president Bolly DeFuze begged Varmint to hold the curtain. Varmint grudgingly agreed, and an announcement was made to the audience. This caused a last-minute stampede to the concession stand.

'You're sure you don't want anything?' Hermux asked Linka. 'I'd be happy to go.'

'I want you right here,' Linka told him. She entwined her fingers in his. 'Besides, we've got to keep an eye on Tucka, haven't we?' She leaned her head close to the Port-a-Pet, which rested on Hermux's shoulder. 'Do you see anything suspicious?' she whispered.

Terfle shook her head, negative. She sat on a stool at the front of her cage, one of her eyes glued to a tiny telescope. The telescope was focused on Tucka, magnifying every detail of her SuperStar costume with such clarity that even the knots in her fur extensions were clearly visible. So far Tucka had done

251

nothing more suspicious than wink at herself in her compact mirror while she touched up her silver lipstick. But the seat next to her was empty, and she was clearly waiting for someone to join her. She was still waiting when the Twyrpian fans arrived and filed noisily into their seats.

As the house lights finally dimmed, Beulith slipped into her seat on the aisle next to Nip.

'Every seat in the house is taken!' she told him excitedly. 'Even standing room is full.'

From the orchestra a solitary oboe began to play 'Happy Birthday,' slowing the tempo and bending the notes until its inherent cheer gave way to a melancholy sense that time was fleeting and that the present would soon be the past.

As the curtain rose, Hermux squeezed Linka's paw and tapped affectionately on Terfle's cage. He leaned forward and waved at Birch and Mirrin, who were sitting nearby. Mirrin gave him a proud thumbs up.

'Good luck!' muttered Hermux. 'We need it!'

From the floor of the stage a circle of columns rose silently into view. A pinpoint of light appeared in the darkness above. It grew brighter and began to move. A pale rat flew through the air. She wore pigtails and firefly wings, and in one hand she held a sparkling wand. She waved her wand as she passed over each column, and it burst into flames. Then she flew away, leaving twenty-five candles burning on the stage.

At the sound of a snare drum, the candles suddenly appeared to grow long, shapely legs. A xylophone kicked a beat. And the chorus-squirrel candles kicked with it. A tuba blared. The circle of kicking candles began to turn like a carousel. Accompanied by the wail of an electric organ, the candles rose up as a turquoise cake emerged from the floor. The string section took up the rhythm. The cake continued to rise, each layer stepping back a notch. At five layers a cymbal crashed. There was a roar from the woodwinds, and the cake lifted off the ground entirely. Jets of popcorn exploded from its base and piled up into mounds. The candles stopped kicking. The cake lurched to a stop. The orchestra fell silent.

Hermux leaned close to Linka.

'This is my favourite part,' he said.

There was a brilliant flash, a puff of smoke, and a doughnut popped from the top layer of the cake like toast from a toaster. One bite of it was missing. The doughnut slowly revolved, and there was Nurella Pinch standing alone in a brilliant white spotlight.

She had on a white sequinned tuxedo and wore a diamond pom-pom at the end of her tail. She sank into a deep curtsy, and the audience released a collective sigh of relief. It was really her. As the realization sank in, the sigh grew into a whooping, foot-stomping cry of joy. Nurella Pinch was back!

When the applause finally subsided, Nurella rose from her curtsy. Tears wet the fur on her face.

'Thank you!' she said. 'I never dreamed I would be here again!'

'Me neither!' shouted someone from the balcony.

And that broke the ice.

Nurella smiled. She snapped her fingers and a crystal goblet appeared in one hand. 'To Fluster Varmint and the Varmint Variety Theatre! To twenty-five years of success! And twenty-five more to come!'

She drank from her glass and tossed it aside.

'I feel like celebrating!' she said.

She snapped her fingers again. A black satin top hat

appeared from nowhere. She popped it open and put it on. She stretched out her right hand. A cane appeared. She twirled it, and a dozen maraschino cherries the size of easy chairs dropped down and made a perfect landing on the cake. She swung her cane through the air and struck it on the side of the doughnut. Everywhere in the theatre, confetti cannons exploded. The cake began to spin again. The squirrels began to kick. The orchestra broke into a toe-tapping medley of her movie themes, and Nurella began to tap her toes. She tapped her way around the cake and up and down its layers. She kicked with the candles. She sang ballads and torch songs. She cracked jokes and told stories. Then the cake descended, telescoping back into the floor and leaving Nurella alone on the stage with the maraschino cherries.

The stage grew dark again, leaving only a single spotlight to illuminate her.

'When I was a little girl,' she told the audience, 'I dreamed of being on a stage just like this. With a theatre full of wonderful people like you. And now I can honestly say that sometimes, dreams really do come true.'

She blew them a kiss.

'It's good to be back,' she said. 'And next time I'll try not to stay away quite so long.' Then she waved. The stage went black.

There was a stunned moment of silence as the curtain fell. Then a roar. Nurella had been there and gone.

Chapter 71
Tucka Gets the Message

Terfle sat back from her telescope and wiped her eye as the house lights came up. She was speechless.

'Wow!' said Nip.

Linka agreed. 'Wow!'

'I think that says it,' said Hermux proudly. He lowered the Port-a-Pet into his lap. 'Are you all right?' he asked Terfle. She answered with a single tap on her bell.

'I hope you'll excuse me,' said Beulith. 'But I'd better get out front and help at the snack bar. It'll be jammed.'

Nip went with her.

'I'm very good with a cash register,' he told her as they vanished into the noisy crowd.

Hermux, Linka and Terfle stayed in their seats and kept their eyes on Tucka. She stayed in her seat too. She had visitors during the interval. Moozella Corkin dropped by to chat. So did Rink. But even from where they were sitting, it was evident to Hermux that Tucka was not her usual self that evening. She seemed uninterested in Moozella. And unamused by Rink's announcement that, after seeing Hermux's set, he would never eat cake again. Tucka fidgeted. She checked her watch. And she watched the door. When the interval ended, she was clearly disappointed and irritated. Her silver lips were clenched in a razor-thin line. Hermux knew that look only too well.

As the lights fell, Nip returned to his seat alone.

'Where's Beulith?' asked Hermux.

'She got called backstage,' he said. 'There's some kind of trouble.'

'What kind?' asked Hermux.

'Something about the ventriloquist.'

Hermux felt a cold chill. But before he could move, the curtain rose. The ventriloquist was onstage.

Dressed in the shiny new suit that Glissin had sewn for him, the shrew faced the audience with a wooden grin and bowed stiffly. On its stand next to him, the parrot bowed too.

There was a smattering of applause.

'Thank you,' said Binter uncomfortably. 'You're beautiful!'

'Yes!' said the parrot, moving its head with an awkward jerk. 'You are a beautiful audience.' The parrot had a raucous and painfully shrill voice. It spoke slowly and mechanically. While it spoke, Binter tried to maintain a fixed and empty smile. But despite strenuous effort, his lips moved. The effect was eerie.

'Should his lips be moving?' Linka whispered to Hermux.

'No,' he whispered back. 'He stinks.'

Then Binter raised his voice a notch and spoke as though he were reading directly from a cue card. 'In fact, we just got word backstage that the most beautiful woman in the world is here tonight.'

'Here and gone!' shouted a heckler.

'No,' said the parrot, using Binter's voice. 'She's in the audience. And she's even more beautiful than Nurella Pinch.'

'Yes!' Binter went on monotonously, using the parrot's voice.

'Even more beautiful than Nurella Pinch.'

'Who?' asked someone.

The parrot turned his head from side to side. His shiny blank eyes scanned the audience. 'She knows who she is.'

After a moment's hesitation, Tucka's hand went up. Hermux sat up in his chair.

'Right!' said the ventriloquist. He directed a spotlight to Tucka. 'There she is! And we've got something special for her tonight! Oh, delivery boy!'

The centre door opened, and the flying squirrel entered at a trot.

'Rush delivery for Tucka Mertslin!' he called out. He proceeded grandly down the aisle, waving to each side as he went. Under one arm he carried a long white box marked ROSES. From the looks of it, it was quite heavy.

'Much too heavy for roses,' thought Hermux. Hermux was moving before he knew it. He thrust the Port-a-Pet at Linka as Terfle hustled to refocus her telescope on the squirrel.

'Where are you going?' Linka asked.

'I've got to stop this!'

'What is it?'

'I don't know. But it's not good.'

'Be careful,' she begged. 'Maybe it's nothing.'

'And maybe not,' said Hermux. 'I can't take the chance.'

He climbed over Nip's lap and ran after the squirrel. 'Give me that box!' Hermux called roughly.

But Tucka had already seen the box. She loved roses. And she was not about to give them up without a fight. She lunged for the aisle, getting to the squirrel a split second before Hermux.

'Those are mine!' she yelled savagely.

Hermux ploughed into the squirrel from behind, fumbled

for a grip, and tried to yank the box away from him. But Tucka grabbed the other end and pulled the other direction. It was a tug-of-war between the watchmaker and the superheroine of beauty. The squirrel was caught in the middle.

'Give me the box!' Hermux implored.

'Can't do it!' said the squirrel. 'They're for the lady!'

'She's no lady!' said Hermux. And as though to prove it, Tucka aimed a violent kick at his shin with her hefty superheroine boot. It connected.

'Ow!' said Hermux. Tucka heaved, and Hermux lost his grip on the box. Tucka, the box and the squirrel flew down the aisle and landed in a heap with the squirrel on top.

'Get off me, you buffoon!' Tucka shoved him away and got to her feet to loud applause. She smiled at the crowd and raised the box above her head in triumph. Then she ripped through the red ribbon with one swipe of her claws and opened it.

Her smile disappeared.

The box was filled with dynamite. It was wired to one of Hermux's own alarm clocks. The alarm was set for 8:50. It was already 8:49.

'On second thoughts,' said Tucka, 'you take it.' She tossed the box to Hermux.

He took one look inside and began to run with it. All he could think of was getting it out of the theatre. He ran up the aisle and out the centre door. He ran past the wishing pond and the grove of birches and out the front entrance on to the street. He looked around desperately for somewhere to dump a bomb. Someplace safe. And then he saw it. Parked across the street.

Tucka's trailer.

He crossed the street, threw open the door, and tossed the bomb inside. Then he dropped down on all fours and ran back

258

towards the theatre as fast as his arms and legs would move.

He made it to the steps before there was a sickening boom, and he found himself lifted from the ground and blown headfirst into the front door. The last thing he saw was a pumpkin-vine hinge coming up fast on his right side.

Chapter 72
MISSING IN ACTION

When Hermux regained consciousness, he found himself on the steps of the theatre. Linka cradled his head in her lap. Her warm paw rested lightly on his forehead. His head ached.

'Are you OK?' she asked tenderly. 'You got quite a wallop.'

'I feel kind of dizzy,' he answered. A circle of concerned faces surrounded him. The situation seemed strangely familiar. 'Why is everyone staring at me? What happened?'

'You saved the theatre,' said Linka. 'You saved all of our lives.' Her voice sounded strangely distant to him.

'I did?' he said. Then it all began to come back to him. The bomb. The running. The explosion. 'Oh. Good.'

'You did a great job!' boomed Varmint. 'Couldn't have done it better myself! Beulith, make a note! Lifetime free tickets for Hermux!'

But Beulith wasn't there. Nip hadn't seen her since the interval. Varmint was just working himself into full hysteria when she appeared in the street. Her beautiful blue party dress was smudged and torn.

All eyes turned on her.

'I heard an explosion,' she said.

Her father ran to her. 'Are you OK? What on earth happened to you?'

'I'm not sure,' she said. 'What happened here?'

'Nothing,' he said. 'Just a bomb.'

'A bomb?' she said in amazement.

'The important thing is that you're OK,' Nip said. 'Where were you?'

'I was tied up,' Beulith said. 'The strangest thing. I got a message at intermission. It was from Binter, the ventriloquist. Some kind of emergency. I went backstage and his apprentice met me. He was acting weird. We had to talk, he said. Outside the theatre. I didn't understand. I didn't want to go. But he forced me. He had a gun!'

'A gun!' Varmint was outraged. 'I'll kill him.'

'No! Let me!' said Nip.

'Dad! Nip! He didn't hurt me.'

'I don't care!'

'Me neither!'

'We walked about a block from here. Then he tied me up. He said he wanted me safe. He said we'd meet again someday. Then he kissed me. And disappeared. Five minutes later, I heard the explosion. A bomb! What does it all mean? What is going on here?'

Hermux had listened carefully. So Crounce had attempted to kill every one of them but his daughter, Beulith. And his plan had almost worked. He was probably getting away at this very minute.

'Where's Terfle?' Hermux asked Linka suddenly.

'Oh, she's fine. That nice mouse from security came and got her, like you asked.'

'What nice mouse?' asked Hermux. 'I didn't ask anyone to get her.'

261

'But he said you had it all planned. If there was an emergency, Terfle was supposed to go to the safe place.'

'What safe place? And Terfle went along with it?'

'I don't know, Hermux! There was an explosion. I wasn't thinking clearly. I was worried about you.'

Hermux struggled to his feet.

'He's got her!' he said.

'Who?'

'Crounce! The ventriloquist's apprentice! He's got Terfle!' Hermux elbowed his way through the crowd, stumbled down the steps, and began to run. He remembered what the squirrel had told him about Crounce. He lived on a boat at the marina.

Hermux had to reach the marina before it was too late.

Chapter 73
HOOK, LINE AND SINKER

Hermux raced to the end of Grandle Street. From its foot a gangplank reached out over the Twisty River and down to the marina. Hermux stopped to catch his breath. In the darkness below he could barely make out the shapes of boats. Downriver a foghorn moaned. Water slapped rhythmically against the hulls of the boats. From somewhere out near the end of the dock came the low, steady throb of an engine.

Hermux crept down the gangplank, wary and alert. When he reached the bottom, he found himself on a narrow, floating dock. On either side the water looked inky black and cold and deep. It pulled and surged and made Hermux a little queasy. He felt his way forward past a houseboat with broken windows and a tugboat that listed to one side. The sound of the engine grew louder. Five yards ahead the marina ended. A low-slung cabin cruiser waited there with its engine idling. Someone stood at the wheel, smoking a cigarette.

The beam of a flashlight caught Hermux full in the face.

'Tantamoq!' It was Crounce. 'I've been waiting for you. Get in the boat!'

'I'm not going anywhere with you!' said Hermux. 'I don't trust you!'

Crounce flicked his cigarette into the river. 'Tsk! Tsk! Then say goodbye to your little friend.' He held up the Port-a-Pet. He raised his other hand. In it was an anchor. The anchor was tied to the Port-a-Pet. He prepared to toss them both overboard. 'Anchors aweigh!' he sang.

'Stop!' shouted Hermux.

'Changed your mind?'

'What do you want?'

'Just to take you for a little spin. I heard you're in the market for a boat!'

Hermux edged his way towards the boat, keeping his eyes on Crounce's hands.

'You heard wrong,' said Hermux. 'Now put her down. The anchor too.'

'As soon as you're safely on board,' replied Crounce. 'I'm familiar with your heroics, remember?'

Hermux grabbed the railing and clambered over. Then he raised his hands over his head. 'See?' he said. 'No tricks.'

Crounce balanced the Port-a-Pet and the anchor on the bulwark. He directed Hermux towards the bench built into the stern. 'Sit down,' he said, waving a snub-nosed pistol. 'And don't try anything stupid.'

'Could you move her cage in a little?' Hermux asked. 'It's awfully close to the edge there.'

Crounce answered with a vicious pull on the throttle. The boat leapt forward, knocking Hermux back against his seat. He watched helplessly as Terfle's cage teetered at the brink. Then, mercifully, at the last second Crounce's hand shot out to steady it. Crounce turned and grinned.

'Comfy?' he asked. The boat continued to gather speed as Crounce guided it towards the main channel. They passed under the High Bridge and skirted the piers, where cargo ships loomed dark against the docks. They rounded the point where the old amusement park stood. Then the river widened out and the city fell away behind them.

'Only ten miles between me and the open sea,' Crounce said.

'A lot can happen in ten miles,' said Hermux under his breath.

'What?' asked Crounce. 'You'll have to speak up. I can't hear you over the engine.'

'I said, "What do you plan to do with us?"'

'Walk the plank! What did you think?'

'I can swim!' boasted Hermux. He knew immediately that he should have kept his mouth shut.

'Good point,' said Crounce. He cut the engine and let the boat drift downstream. He levelled the gun at Hermux again. 'You can do a lot of things, can't you? Minding your own business does not seem to be one of them. Too bad for you!'

'Listen, there's no reason to hurt Terfle,' Hermux bargained. 'She didn't do anything to you.'

Crounce peered into her cage. 'Is that right?' he asked. 'Innocent?'

Terfle refused to answer.

'What did you have in mind?' Crounce asked Hermux.

'Let her go, and I'll cooperate.'

'Will you?'

'Things will go a lot easier.'

'Things would go easier if I just shot you right now.'

'That's true,' said Hermux. Then he had an idea. 'But it wouldn't be as much fun, would it?'

Crounce's perfect smile appeared ghostly in the moonlight.

'You have a point there.'

'Good. Then we have an agreement. You promise me that Terfle will go free and unharmed. And I'll do whatever you want.'

'Promise.'

'All right, then. What do you want me to do?'

Crounce tossed him a coil of rope. 'Tie this around your feet.'

Hermux tied it.

'Tighter.'

Reluctantly Hermux tightened the knot.

'Now throw me the other end. You couldn't keep your big nose out of it, could you?' Crounce pocketed his gun and threaded the rope through the ring of the anchor. 'Everything would have gone smoothly. I'd be rid of them all now. I'd be rid of you too, for that matter. But I'm getting to that.' He knotted the rope and tested it. 'There! Nice and snug.'

He prepared to throw the anchor overboard.

'Wait a minute!' Hermux demanded. 'Untie Terfle's cage. That was part of the bargain!'

'Bargain?' asked Crounce. 'I don't remember bargaining.'

'You're a liar!'

'Now! Now! I wouldn't want your last words to be spoken in anger.'

Inside the Port-a-Pet a bell began to ring. It had a light, silvery sound.

'Now, what does she want?' Crounce asked irritably. He peered into the cage. A brilliant flash of colour caught his eye. 'What's she doing?' It flashed again. And again.

On. And off.

On. And off.

On. And off.

266

It was very pleasant to look at. And listening to the bell was pleasant too. It was all very relaxing. Not like the frustrating day he had just had trying to kill Nurella, Tucka, and half of Pinchester.

Terfle held the sequin between her forelegs, focusing the moonlight and directing it up at Crounce. With one hindleg she tapped a slow and sinuous rhythm on the emergency bell.

Crounce stood very still. Hermux recognized the symptoms.

'You must be tired,' Hermux spoke in a slow, calm and soothing voice. 'You're very, very tired. And when you're tired, isn't it pleasant to just let yourself go? Isn't it nice to forget about all your cares and worries and simply focus your mind on the pretty light? The way it flashes and shines. The way it sparkles. Isn't it a lovely colour? So, so soothing. So, so reassuring.'

Crounce's eyes were fixed and glassy. Hermux moved very slowly. Still talking, he leaned forward and began to untie his feet.

'Now just let yourself relax and feel the gentle rocking of the boat. Moving back and forth. And back and forth.' Hermux's voice droned on. 'Letting go of everything that's holding you down. Letting go of the knots. Letting go of the ties that bind. Now let's remove the rope from the cage.'

Crounce untied the Port-a-Pet.

'That's it. That feels so much better. Now, isn't there something in your pocket that's weighing you down? A burden that's heavy to carry. It's time to let it go. Take it out. *Careful!* And let it drop to the floor.'

Crounce took out the gun and dropped it.

'There!' breathed Hermux. 'Doesn't that feel better? Now kick it away from you and forget all about it.'

Crounce kicked the gun towards Hermux. As he did, the

boat gave a lurch. Crounce was thrown off balance. As he struggled to regain his footing, he snapped out of his trance. He jerked his gun hand up and found, to his surprise, that it was empty. Then Hermux lunged for the pistol. Instinctively Crounce lunged for Hermux. They collided midair and tumbled across the deck, punching and scratching. Hermux broke free and scrabbled forward on his hands and knees. He had the gun in his grasp when Crounce landed a flying two-footed kick in the small of his back. Hermux went down hard. The gun skidded hopelessly out of his reach. As Hermux struggled to breathe again, Crounce knelt easily and retrieved it.

Watching from her perch in the Port-a-Pet, Terfle stifled a hopeless sob.

'Nice try,' said Crounce.

Hermux didn't answer. He needed a weapon. Then he saw the rope.

'I'm not sure which one of you to kill first,' Crounce gloated. 'I suppose it makes the most sense to eat the bug and make you watch. That would be amusing. Then I can shoot you.' As Crounce turned towards the Port-a-Pet, Hermux grabbed the rope, tied a slipknot, pulled it open, and threw it out on the deck like a lasso. Now he needed time. And some luck.

'What was your plan, anyway?' Hermux asked. 'Once we were all dead? I'm sure it was brilliant!'

Crounce stopped. It *was* a brilliant plan. And he'd never get to tell anyone else.

'You really want to know?'

'I'm dying to,' said Hermux. He concentrated as hard as he could. 'Two steps back,' he prayed. 'Just two steps.'

Crounce took a step towards him.

'I would have waited. Six months. A year. The time would

have passed pleasantly just knowing that Varmint and Nurella were both dead – that they had paid the price for keeping me from being a star. Then I would have come back.'

'To console the grieving daughter?'

'To help the heiress get over her loss. Money has its advantages.'

'As opposed to love?'

'Was it love to let her grow up in a second-rate theatre with a buffoon for a father?'

'You mean instead of a murderer?'

'You know, you can be very irritating,' said Crounce. 'At least I'm going to have the satisfaction of seeing you suffer.' He took another step. Inside the rope.

That was all Hermux needed. Quick as lightning he rolled sideways, bounced off the stern, and scrambled forward. But Crounce was quick too. He raised the gun and fired. Once. Twice. Hermux dodged left and right, counting the shots and hoping against hope. Crounce fired again. And missed again. Another and Hermux felt a searing pain midway down his tail. He stumbled to the wheel, cornered now.

Crounce took steady aim.

'So long, Tantamoq!'

Terfle rang her bell indignantly.

'Shut up!' Crounce snarled. He pointed the gun at the Port-a-Pet and squeezed the trigger. The door exploded in splinters. That was enough for Hermux. He grabbed the rope and yanked, snaring Crounce by the ankles.

'Still one more bullet!' Crounce taunted.

As Crounce aimed again, Hermux pushed the anchor overboard and gunned the throttle. Crounce's shot went wild. Then the rope went taut. Crounce's feet lifted clear off the deck.

And the boat jumped forward, leaving Crounce behind. There was a splash. And the black water swallowed him whole.

Hermux killed the throttle. As the boat slowed, he reached for the Port-a-Pet and cradled it tenderly in his arms.

'Terfle!' he murmured. 'Please be OK.'

There was a faint rustle in response. Then one black feeler poked out of the shattered door. Followed by another.

Chapter 74
ALL WRAPPED UP

The next morning, Hermux and Terfle slept in. They slept right through lunch and might have slept through dinner if the doorbell hadn't awakened them.

Hermux answered in his pyjamas.

It was the flying squirrel.

'Oh, no!' thought Hermux. 'Here we go again!'

The flying squirrel handed Hermux a large, heavy box tied with a red ribbon. 'This one's on the house,' he said, and left without another word.

Hermux carried the box into the den.

There was a note attached.

VARMINT VARIETY THEATRE

To Hermux and Terfle,
Many thanks from all your friends and fans
at the theatre!

Everyone had signed it.

Inside the box was a brand-new Port-a-Pet Palace. Fully loaded. And fully furnished. It even had a make-up table, a mirror and lights.

There was also a copy of the *Daily Sentinel* with a photo of Hermux and Terfle on the front page. Right next to the picture of Nurella Pinch. In the picture Terfle's shell was bandaged. So was Hermux's tail. Terfle had two splits, a nick and a serious dent from the emergency-bell shrapnel. Hermux had eleven stitches. They both looked tired. But proud. And glad to be alive.

'It's time for us to get up and get out,' said Hermux.

Terfle was dressed and ready to go in less than five minutes. It took Hermux a little longer. It wasn't easy taking a shower or putting on trousers with a wounded tail.

Their first stop was the theatre.

Varmint was in his office. He was glad to see them, but he couldn't talk. He was in an emergency production meeting with Beulith, Oaf, Sputter, Gnawton and Chizzel. They were planning the next show. A murder mystery about a psychotic ventriloquist who terrorizes a theatre.

'Great parts for both of you!' Varmint promised. Then he closed the door.

'I guess the show must go on,' said Hermux, somewhat disappointed. 'Let's go see Glissin. Maybe she has time for us. Besides, I have something to give her.'

They found Glissin in her studio, fitting a giant daisy hat on to a squirrel mannequin's head. Her face lit up when she saw them. 'Just a sec,' she said. She adjusted the stiff white petals and trimmed away a few loose threads. ' "Waltz of the Flowers". What do you think? Varmint wants a new number in the second act.'

Her worktable was littered with sketches of petunias and snapdragons. She showed Terfle swatches of the fabrics she was considering for stems and leaves. Terfle favoured the bright green silk.

'Me too,' said Glissin happily. 'I knew we'd agree.' Then she turned serious. 'I'll never be able to thank you two enough. Never. You saved us all. Everything that matters. And to think that you were nearly killed!'

'Several times,' said Hermux. It seemed important to mention.

'But you're both OK?' Glissin looked at them with concern.

Terfle showed off her bandages.

'On the mend,' said Hermux.

'I'm very sorry.'

'But it wasn't your fault,' said Hermux.

'It was me he blamed.'

'He blamed everyone,' said Hermux. 'Everyone but himself. He taught me something about revenge, at least. Regardless of what they say, it's not sweet at all. Give me a doughnut any day. And speaking of treats, we have something for you.' He handed Glissin a small box.

She opened it. It was her wristwatch with the masks of Comedy and Tragedy.

'It keeps perfect time,' explained Hermux. 'I completely rebuilt it.'

Glissin lifted the watch delicately. She held it to her ear and listened to its smooth, regular tick. She put it on her wrist and showed it off.

'How do I look?' she asked.

She looked kind, calm and competent. No one would ever

guess that she was the same mouse who had got a standing ovation and seventeen curtain calls the night before.

'Incidentally,' said Hermux in a low voice, 'that was a wonderful performance last night. Thank you!'

'Don't thank me. Thank Nurella. She did all the work.'

'Well, if you should happen to see her,' said Hermux with a twinkle in his eye, 'please thank her for me. I understand she left before anyone got a chance to say goodbye.'

'I will thank her. I think she enjoyed herself,' Glissin said. 'Who knows? Maybe she'll be back.'

'And Beulith?' asked Hermux. 'Did you tell her?'

'Almost. But then I asked myself, would I be telling her for her sake? Or for mine?'

'I see what you mean,' said Hermux. 'It's hard to know.'

'Maybe someday,' said Glissin. 'But there's no hurry any more. Thanks to you and to Terfle.'

'It was our pleasure,' said Hermux. And he meant it.

'And so?' asked Glissin. 'What's in the future for Hermux Tantamoq? Back to watchmaking? You're sure you won't miss us?'

'I've got to make a living,' said Hermux. 'Besides, I do love watches.'

'I'm going to miss you, Hermux. And Terfle, of course. I wonder –'

'Yes?'

'The theatre is not far out of your way, is it?'

'Oh, I plan to visit regularly,' Hermux assured her.

'That's not it,' said Glissin. 'Of course you're always welcome. But really I was wondering about Terfle. She and I work so well together. And she does seem to get a bit lonely when you're working. I was wondering if you might drop her by on your way to the shop. She and I could spend the days together. She's a big help to me.'

Hermux was taken by surprise. 'It's an interesting idea.' He hesitated. 'But it would be up to Terfle, not me.'

Terfle's bell rang loud and clear.

'And there's your answer,' said Hermux. 'It looks like you have a new assistant.'

Chapter 75
THE CALL OF THE WILD

Leaving the Varmint Variety Theatre that afternoon, Hermux felt a bit of a let-down. It had been a most excellent adventure to be sure. But now it was over.

'Adventure gives a person a sense of purpose,' Hermux observed.

Terfle agreed.

Hermux walked towards Orsik & Arrbale, pausing to look up at the towering buildings that lined the avenue. He observed the bustle of people streaming in and out of the big department store. Everyone seemed to be on a mission of some sort.

'And you meet very interesting people on an adventure. We certainly met our share on this one.'

Terfle agreed with that too.

Hermux stopped at Orsik & Arrbale's corner window and watched two wiry chipmunks attach a Tucka Mertslin action figure on the back of a lipstick rocket ship orbiting the planet Earth. Above streamed a legend in Day-Glo letters.

Only one beauty can save the world!

SUPERSTAR!

The Explosive New Lipstick From Tucka Mertslin

Hermux sighed and moved on to the next window. He leaned his forehead against the cold glass and closed his eyes. He pictured himself back in his shop, waiting for a mysterious aviatrix to rush through the door with a broken watch. Or waiting for a one-eared chipmunk to arrive with a strange secret. Or a flying squirrel to deliver a message from a theatrical impresario.

'I hope we get another adventure soon,' he said. 'The waiting part is what gets me down.'

Terfle listened sympathetically.

Then Hermux opened his eyes. Before him in the window was a bed of moss. On the moss sat a nest made of tiny twigs. And in the nest was a gold ring with a glowing dark red stone.

Beside it sat a small white card. It said:

Why not ask her today!

Hermux blinked and swallowed. 'Why not, indeed?' he thought. He pictured the ring on Linka's hand. He pictured Linka at his side.

Terfle rang her bell encouragingly.

'You're right!' said Hermux. 'We can wait for adventure to come to us. Or we can go look for it ourselves.'